"Here they come!" Link cried, as a blast of rifle fire hit the building. The men and Annie turned to the windows and doors. Kimball hid under the table. Through his window shutter, Lieutenant Tom Conroy saw shapes all around in the darkness, rushing the station house.

"Fire!" he yelled.

Soldiers and civilians opened up. There were flashes in the darkness, drifting powder smoke, screams from outside. The din in the small building was tremendous. The two parties were trading shots at almost point-blank range.

"Find some ammunition! We're almost out!" Tom cried.

"There isn't any more!" Bisonette yelled back. "It blew up with the storeroom!"

Beneath the crackle of gunfire came a deeper, heavier sound—the rumbling of a flaming wagon stuffed with dry prairie grass that the Indians were rolling straight for the door.

Also by Robert W. Broomall
Published by Fawcett Books:

THE BANK ROBBER
DEAD MAN'S CANYON
DEAD MAN'S CROSSING
DEAD MAN'S TOWN
TEXAS KINGDOMS
CALIFORNIA KINGDOMS
K COMPANY
THE LAWMEN

CONROY'S FIRST COMMAND

Robert W. Broomall

FAWCETT GOLD MEDAL • NEW YORK

A Fawcett Crest Book
Published by Ballantine Books
Copyright © 1994 by Robert W. Broomall

Library of Congress Catalog Card Number: 94-94041

ISBN 0-449-14857-2

Printed in Canada

First Edition: July 1994

10 9 8 7 6 5 4 3 2 1

1

"To the rear—march!"

Harry Winston took one step too many, pivoting on his left foot instead of his right and colliding with the last three men in the file, who had done the movement correctly. Off by the row of tents that formed one side of the improvised parade ground, the watching civilians hooted with derision as the soldiers struggled back into line.

Link Hayward was on top of Harry right away. "Winston, you sorry sack of shit. How did you ever get in the army?"

Harry tried to regain his place in line and keep marching, but Link wouldn't let him. "Get out of my formation," he ordered. "Get that weapon over your head. Who told the rest of you people to stop marching? Start running, Winston. If you can't march in this formation, you can run around it."

With the seven-shot Spencer carbine over his head, Harry began double-timing around the file of four men as Link led them across the Buffalo Creek Station parade ground. The August sun beat down on the dusty piece of West Kansas prairie.

"Hut! Hut! Hut, two, three, four. Hut! Hut! To the left—march!"

Harry struggled to keep up, cursing Link under his breath.

"Shut up, Winston, or I'll have you strung up by the thumbs."

1

Link would do it, too. Harry kept running, wondering why he had ever joined the army. Sweat dripped from beneath his wool forage cap. The shoulder that had been wounded at Cheyenne Bluff started to ache.

"Right flank—march!" Link ordered.

From beyond the line of picketed horses that comprised another side of the parade ground came a cry. "Corporal of the guard!"

Link turned to watch as Skull Anders left the guard tent and started across the parade ground, still gimpy from the hip wound he had received at Cheyenne Bluff. One of Link's men turned, too. "What are you looking at, McIlhargy?" Link bellowed. "Are you the corporal of the guard?"

"No, Sergeant . . ."

"You chowderheaded Paddy, get out here. Get that weapon over your head. Now start doing knee bends."

The red-haired Irishman hoisted his Spencer and began doing deep knee bends, while Link led his depleted squad through its drills. "Your left. Your left. Your left, right, left. Left flank—march!"

The civilians from the station were enjoying the spectacle immensely, laughing and jeering. "Watch out, Sarge," yelled one. "You got yourself some real killers there."

"Thought you boys were cavalry," shouted another. "How come you're doing infantry drills?"

" 'Cause they can't ride," said the first, and the civilians all laughed.

"You better learn to march," cried a buckskinned fellow named Hicks, " 'cause everybody knows you can't fight."

Link turned and fixed Hicks with a cold stare. "Ignore those bastards," he told his men, turning back. "They're civilians. Hut! Hut! Any asshole can be a civilian, it takes a man to be a soldier. Your left, right, left. Not that any of you are soldiers, but you may be before you leave K Company. Squad—halt! Left—face! Order—arms!"

Link put his three remaining men through the manual of arms, while Harry kept running around them and McIlhargy did knee bends, the strain showing on his freckled face. The three men performed the movements with varying degrees of smartness, led by Frazer, who had fought in the war and was an accomplished parade ground soldier. From the corner of his eye Link saw the guard go to Lieutenant Conroy's tent, bringing the C.O. out to look at whatever was going on beyond the horse lines. A few minutes later the guard, whose name was Moonlight, came for Link. "Sergeant Hayward—Lieutenant Conroy wants you."

"Very well," Link said. He barked, "Squad, order—arms! At—ease! Nobody told you to stop running, Winston! When I get back, I expect you and McIlhargy to still be exercising. The rest of you remain as you are."

Link accompanied Moonlight across the parade ground, past the horse lines. He moved briskly but unhurriedly, his forage cap tilted over his eyes. Lieutenant Conroy and Skull stood by the haystack, gazing west.

"Yes, sir?" Link asked, but he saw right away why the lieutenant had sent for him.

"Squaw camp's moving," Conroy said.

"Yes, sir." Squaw camp was the name given to the semipermanent village of friendly Indians, mainly Cheyenne and Arapaho, who had come to the station to trade. Now, at mid-morning, the Indian women were hurriedly taking down the lodges, bundling infants and parfleches on travois, while the camp dogs barked and men and boys rounded up the horses.

The fair-haired young lieutenant looked at Link. He wore a beautifully tailored uniform—dark blue shell jacket, sky-blue trousers, white shirt. His ankle boots and cap visor gleamed. "You've been on the prairie before, Sergeant. What do you make of it?"

Link stood with his hands behind his back. "Don't know, sir. Could be they've been here long enough, and it's time to move on." He paused. "Could be there's going to be trouble."

Lieutenant Conroy thought for a second, then he said, "Have our horses saddled, Sergeant."

2

Tom Conroy and Sergeant Hayward rode across Buffalo Creek and up a rise on the far side. From this point they had a sweeping view across the sagebrush-covered prairie. Tom had put on soft brown riding gloves. He took his field glasses from their case and scanned the countryside. He could see for maybe thirty miles in every direction. The prairie was like an ocean—vast, rolling, and eternal—broken only by the tree- and brush-covered lines of the Smoky Hill River, just to the south, and of Buffalo Creek, which flowed into it. Tom paused the glasses on a distant dust cloud, which proved to be an antelope herd. Coming full circle, he saw his platoon's grazing horse herd. Beyond that was the rectangular outline of his small tent camp, dubbed Camp Conroy, then the stage station and its outbuildings. Downstream he could see the cattle belonging to the station's owner, Bisonette. Stretching into the hazy distance to east and west were the emigrant road and the telegraph poles that ran beside it.

Tom lowered the glasses and handed them to Hayward. "I don't see anything."

"You probably wouldn't, sir, not if there was going to be trouble."

"There's been nothing over the telegraph. This is supposed to be a quiet area. The Comanches and Kiowas are south of the Arkansas. The hostile Cheyennes and their allies are up around the forks of the Republican, with Custer and the Seventh on their trail."

Tom stopped. He'd said more than he should have. There was more that he wanted to say and to ask, but he couldn't. The gulf between officers and enlisted men did not permit such familiarity. As an officer, it was Tom's job to remain remote and aloof. There were very few officers who could break that barrier and still be efficient. Jim Starke, K Company's acting C.O., had the knack, but Tom knew that he would never possess it.

While Link took a turn with the field glasses, Tom looked back at his camp. Link's drill squad was still standing rigidly at ease, with two of the men doing some kind of punishment. This morning's drill was the first since Tom and his platoon had arrived at Buffalo Creek, two weeks ago. After what the papers were calling the Battle of Cheyenne Bluff, K Company—what was left of it—had returned to Fort Pierce. Once there, the C.O., Captain Bannerman, had hurriedly departed on recruiting duty in the East, taking his wife Helene with him and leaving Lieutenant Starke in temporary command. Replacements had arrived just as the company was ordered to provide a detachment for the stage station at Buffalo Creek. With the fall buffalo hunt at hand, most of the Indian raiding should have ended, so Starke had thought this would be a good chance to give Tom some experience at independent command.

Their mission was to guard the station and to escort stagecoaches from the station to Cheyenne Wells, a day's ride to the west. To do that, Tom had sixteen mostly inexperienced privates, two corporals, and Sergeant Hayward. Of this group, a corporal and four men were always on detached service as stage escort. The other corporal and four more men were needed to post guard. An additional man was detailed for cookhouse duty and another to guard the horse herd. That left Tom with six privates for everything else—from pursuing Indian raiders, to water hauling, hay and wood cutting, and construction of winter quarters for themselves and stables for the horses. And that was if no one was sick or in the guard tent. The men were forced to work on Sundays. Those coming off guard received no rest. Military routine was limited to roll calls and daily inspections.

Tom's only consolation was that this schedule left his men little time to get in trouble with Bisonette and the woolly characters who frequented his station. The men had no money to spend there in any case—they had not been paid since just before taking the field against Chief Storm and his Cheyennes last May.

Now that the squaw camp was leaving, Tom would no longer have to try and keep his men from sneaking in there and seeking the favors of the Indian women. He also wouldn't have to worry about the Indians stealing his horses' corn and anything else that wasn't tied down.

And if there was trouble?

Tom had proved himself in the battle at Cheyenne Bluff, but he had yet to prove himself in command. He knew that the men doubted him; the truth was, he doubted himself. He wasn't a West Pointer or a Civil War veteran; he was a political appointee, a rich boy who had gotten his place because of his father's connections. He wondered if he could cut it.

Sergeant Hayward put down the field glasses. Tall, spare, and dark, in his early thirties, Hayward had been in the army since before the war. There wasn't much that he hadn't seen, and there wasn't much that could surprise him. He returned the expensive field glasses, and Tom put them back in their leather case. Tom felt uneasy around his sergeant. Hayward had a reputation for drunkenness and insubordination. The sergeant hadn't given him any trouble yet, but there was always a glint in his eye, an insolent upturn to one corner of his mouth, to suggest that he might.

Tom said, "What's your assessment of the situation, Sergeant?"

"Don't know, sir. The rule of thumb in Indian fighting is that you can expect to fire your weapon in anger once in a five-year hitch. By that measure, we've seen a career's worth of action already this summer. Still . . ." He watched the friendly Indian camp heading west in the direction of Big Timbers. "I don't know, sir. I've got a funny feeling about this one."

Tom nodded, and Hayward went on. "Bit of advice, sir?"

"Yes?" Tom said.

Hayward spoke respectfully, locking his gaze onto some unseen middle ground. "You're too tentative, sir, you're too worried about doing bad. Don't second-guess yourself. Don't be afraid to command. Once you make a decision, forget about whether it was right or not and go on to the next one. The worst that can happen is that we all get killed, and that's our job anyway. It ain't like we're going to decide the fate of the world out here, you know. So just go ahead and have fun with it."

"Fun?" Tom cleared his throat. "Hm, thank you, Sergeant. I hadn't thought of it in quite that way. Very well—instruct the guards to be alert for trouble, especially the herd guards." He would have liked to redouble the guards, but he didn't have enough men. "Take your detail to dinner, then put them to work on the stables for the afternoon."

"Yes, sir," the sergeant replied.

Stretching in his McClellan saddle, Tom took a last look around the prairie—so wide, unknown, and suddenly threatening. He thought about what Jim Starke had said to him just before he left for Buffalo Creek: "No matter how long you're in the army, or how far you go, you'll always remember your first command."

Tom nodded to himself—he could believe that. Then he and Sergeant Hayward rode back to the station.

3

"You think these stables will be ready by winter?" McIlhargy asked.

"Yeah," Harry said. "The winter of 1880."

The mid-afternoon sun beat down. The breeze had died to a whisper. Flies buzzed in hungry swarms. Harry was stretched in the shade, reclined against the half-finished stable wall. Nine months in the army had taught him to get sleep whenever and wherever he could.

Around him, the other men worked listlessly in the heat. Like Harry, they had doffed their blue fatigue jackets. McIlhargy lifted an adobe brick from the pile and set it in place on the wall with a cement made from bull's blood. The redheaded Irishman was rubbery-legged from the morning's knee bends. There was a note of urgency in his voice. "This is no time to be sleepin', Harry. We can't build our winter quarters till we're done here. It gets bloody cold on these plains, so Oi'm told."

"There's no rush," Harry assured him, with his eyes closed. Harry was tired from double-timing, and his shoulder ached. "Who says there'll be a garrison here till winter? And even if there is, who says it'll be us? They might pull us out and put another outfit in. Let them worry about freezing."

"My, my, aren't you the old soldier?" said a fresh voice.

Harry opened his eyes. "Hunter. What are you doing here?"

"Looking for Link. He around?"

"He's over at the guard tent, with Skull."

Hunter snorted. "They're probably thinking up a way to get whiskey. All that booze at the station, and us without a penny to buy it. I wish Starving Mike's allowance would come through."

"Starving Mike" was what they had called Steroverovka, a Russian who had been killed at Cheyenne Bluff. Mike had claimed descent from a long line of czarist army officers, and he periodically received money from home. A bank draft had come for him just before the platoon had left for Buffalo Creek. Lieutenant Starke had allowed the men to cash it, and Link and the veterans had used it to go on a monumental drunk.

"Maybe somebody told his family he's dead," Harry suggested.

"Why would they do that?" Hunter asked. "We need the money more than they do."

Harry changed the subject. "Aren't you supposed to be working?"

Hunter flashed his infectious smile. "I'm on police call. Pulling weeds around the tents. It's all I can do with one hand." He showed his right hand, on the back of which was a puckered, whitish scar.

Harry shook his head. Because of his bad hand, Hunter was restricted to permanent orderly and other light duties. "I can't believe Boy Wonder is falling for your bullshit a second time."

"It's no bullshit," Hunter insisted. "I was faking it before, but this time I'm not. Since I got shot again at Cheyenne Bluff, I've got no play with this hand. It's stiff and numb. It's got me worried, Mad Dog. I'm afraid I might lose it."

"Did you put in for a discharge again?"

Hunter wrinkled his brow. "Not yet, but I don't see what else I can do."

"And if you get one, you'll come back again, like you did last time."

"Not me. Next time, I'm gone for good. The company

ain't the same no more. Except for you and Link and a
few others, all my friends are gone—the Arab, Jack
Cassaday, Mick Bannon, Amassee. Anyway, I can't
come back—I'm crippled."

George Frazer, the smooth ex–Civil War officer, had
been listening. He said, "Can I ask you something? How
come everybody calls you Hunter, when your real name
is Campbell?"

"I must have misspelled it on my enlistment papers,"
Hunter told him.

Nearby, Frank Walsh, the twenty-year-old Bowery
tough, looked around, then slipped a deck of cards from
his pocket. "Anybody for some poker? We can play
against our next payday, whenever that is. What do you
say, Hunter—want to play?"

"Drop dead, Streak," Hunter told him.

"I'll play," George Frazer said.

The two men sat in the shade. Only Shorty Ewing and
McIlhargy still made a pretense of working. Walsh shuf-
fled the cards and dealt. The men used stones for coins.
"Man, I hate to see that squaw camp leave," Walsh said.
"Now where do we go to get laid?"

"Try one of Bisonette's cows," Hunter told him. "You
wouldn't know the difference."

Walsh ignored him, scratching a flea bite on his cheek.
"I really liked that little Arapaho bitch called Dove. Any
of you ever try her? Man, she'd do just about anything."

"Including give you the clap," Hunter said. "You and
anybody else dumb enough to mess with Injun women."

Shorty Ewing, a former grocer from Washington,
D.C., stretched his stiff back. "God, I'm tired. When do
we get to do some real soldiering, anyway? I didn't join
up to be a construction worker. I could have done that at
home. All this building—why can't we stay at the station
this winter? Bisonette's got room up there."

"He says he doesn't," Harry told him. "It's his station."

"Ungrateful French bastard," Walsh said. "We're protecting him, ain't we?"

"Protecting him from what?" Frazer asked. "There's no Indians around here. All we're doing is make-work jobs—escorting stages and pulling guard. And when you don't have those, you're on fatigue, like now. I can't remember the last time I got a decent night's rest."

Walsh agreed. "The army sucks big dicks."

"That makes two of you," Hunter told him.

Walsh looked up darkly. "You're lucky you're a cripple, Hunter."

Frazer won the hand, raked in his winning of stones, and drew more cards. "One thing is certain—our shavetail lieutenant doesn't know the first thing about running a company."

"I guess *you* do?" Hunter said.

"Yes, as a matter of fact. I commanded a company during the war. As a major, I commanded a battalion."

"Yeah, yeah. If you were so great, how come you're a private now?"

Frazer was philosophical. "Certain business ventures in civilian life didn't work out. I intend to regain my commission before long."

"Good luck," Hunter cracked.

"I would certainly do better than Wonder Boy Conroy," Frazer said. "And as an experienced combat officer, I have better claim to a commission."

McIlhargy wiped his sweaty brow. "What do *you* think of the lieutenant, Hunter?"

Hunter shrugged. "Hard to say. I know one thing—he ain't yellow, like Streak here."

"I ain't yellow," Walsh growled.

"You sure gave a good imitation of it at Cheyenne Bluff," Hunter told him.

Harry laughed.

"Shut up, Mad Dog," Walsh said.

Harry stood. "Why don't you make me, Streak?" His

belligerent reaction surprised even himself. Hunter was right—the army had changed him.

"Keep calling me yellow, and I will make you," Walsh swore. He still remembered when everyone picked on Harry, and he thought he could bully him.

"I'm calling you yellow now," Harry said.

Walsh rose as well. "Watch yourself, Winston."

"Break it up," Hunter hissed. "The lieutenant's coming."

The rest of the men scrambled to their feet, brushing their trousers and coming to attention, as Lieutenant Conroy came over. "What's going on here? Where is Sergeant Hayward?"

"Here, sir," Link said, appearing at the lieutenant's elbow as if by magic.

"Why aren't these men working?" Conroy asked him.

Link stood at attention. "They were taking a break, sir."

Conroy looked around. "Judging by the amount of work that's been done on these stables, the break has lasted all afternoon."

"The men *are* tired, sir. Some of 'em ain't had no sleep."

Conroy wasn't sure how to reply. His eye lighted on Hunter. "This man isn't part of your detail. What's he doing here?"

Hunter answered. "I needed to ask the sergeant something, sir."

Conroy rubbed a hand across his clean-shaven jaw, then saw the playing cards scattered on the ground. "Were you men gambling on duty?"

"Oh, no, sir," Walsh said hastily. "We was just playing for fun, like. For practice."

"I'll have those cards, Sergeant."

"Yes, sir," Link said. He nodded to Walsh. Walsh scraped up the cards and gave them to Link, who in turn handed them to Conroy.

"Set these men to work," Conroy ordered, pocketing the deck of cards. "And keep an eye on them."

Link saluted crisply. "Yes, sir." He looked around. "You heard the lieutenant. These stables ain't going to build themselves. Move it! *Achi bat!* as Sergeant Townsend used to say."

The men went back to work, stacking the adobe bricks on the stable wall, one row lengthwise, the next row crosswise. Conroy watched for a few minutes, then left, heading for the tent that served as a company office.

As soon as he was gone, the men relaxed, leaning against the wall. Harry lay down and went to sleep.

4

In front of the guard tent, O'Meara—appointed trumpeter because he knew a bit about music—sounded recall from stables, and the men returned from the horse lines to get ready for supper.

Tom Conroy left his tent, straightening his shell jacket and putting on his forage cap. Tom's quarters were across the parade ground from the men's. He had two wall tents connected by a canvas fly. One tent was his accommodation, the other was an office where he did the unit paperwork. There was a camp chair and table beneath the fly, where he would sit in the evenings and read or simply relax.

Tom crossed the parade ground, returning the salutes of his men. He turned up the emigrant road toward the stage station, a few hundred yards to the east, where he took his meals, contracted for by the government. The road was deeply rutted and littered with a decade's worth of garbage. There was no grass left within two hundred yards on either side. Now that the war was over, westbound traffic was heavier than ever. And next year or the year after, the railroad would come through.

Tom paused and looked west in the golden light of late afternoon, toward the creek ford and the plain beyond. He breathed deeply, smelling the prairie sage and wild plums, listening to the sigh of the breeze that came all the way from Canada. He tried to fix the scene in his mind's eye—the setting sun, the endless expanse of wilderness. He wanted to remember it, because he knew that soon it would be gone. The time of the Indian and buffalo was nearly past. They were about to give way to the plow and the settler, the merchant and the town. One day it would be as if this wild land and its wild inhabitants had never existed. Tom was doing his part in hastening that day. Sometimes he wondered if he was doing the right thing.

He turned back and crossed the road. Buffalo Creek Station consisted of two adobe houses, one used by Bisonette as a residence, the other as a stage station and store. The two houses were connected by a gate, which provided entrance to a stockaded corral, inside of which were stables, a blacksmith shop, kitchen, and storehouse. Across from the station was the telegraph relay office, along with the shacks and dugouts that served as living quarters for the other men who worked here.

There was a rack of elk antlers over the station-house entrance; rough laughter floated out the open door. Tom stepped in, tucking his cap under his arm. The station had a low-ceilinged interior, with a crude bar against one wall and a long table down the center, where the stage passengers took their meals. There were other tables in the corners, and shelves with store goods along the walls. There were half a dozen men inside. Five were playing poker. The sixth, Nilsson the blacksmith, sat alone in the far corner, drinking.

Tom had never been in the station when there wasn't a poker game going. He sometimes thought the game never stopped, that only the players changed. Right now a bearded, shady-looking character was raising like mad. Tom had seen the man around the station before. He claimed to be a lumber cutter, but if he had ever been near an axe or ripsaw, Tom suspected it had been by accident. While Tom watched, the "lumber cutter" raised everyone out of the hand except for the station owner, Jules Bisonette. Pipe jutting from a corner of his mouth, Bisonette matched the lumber cutter raise for raise, until at last the man called.

One by one Bisonette turned over his cards. He had a jack high.

The lumber cutter's jaw flapped open.

"And you?" Bisonette said confidently. He was a heavyset man in his late thirties, just under six feet tall. His dark hair and beard were turning gray, and there were deep lines around his eyes. He wore a checked wool shirt and fringed elkskin pants.

The lumber cutter showed his hand. He had nothing, either—a nine of hearts was his high card. "How did you know I was bluffing?" he asked.

"I didn't," Bisonette said, grinning. "I always bet on the jack. It's my lucky card. It's never been a loser for me."

"That's right," Hicks agreed, Bisonette's second in charge at the station. "Hell, I seen ol' Jules stake this station on a pair of jacks."

The lumber cutter shook his head and poured a drink, while Bisonette raked in his considerable winnings. He looked up and saw Tom. "Hello, soldier boy. Come for your supper?"

Tom shifted uneasily. "That's right."

Bisonette stood. "Deal me out," he told the other players. With his pipe, he indicated the long table. "Have a seat, sonny. I'll get your food."

Tom moved to the table. The men in the room were

smiling at him. "Hey, Lieutenant," Hicks shouted, "tell that big sergeant of yours to watch his mouth. It's liable to get him in trouble." Hicks was a wiry fellow, about ten years younger than Bisonette, with long hair, a moustache, and goatee. He was said to be a wanted criminal in the States. He was dressed in deerskins, with two pistols in deerskin holsters—every man in the room except Tom had at least one pistol in his belt.

Tom sat, while the card players discussed the departure of the squaw camp. "My woman went with them," Hicks complained. "Damn strange, the way it happened. Up and left, she did, without so much as a fare-thee-well. Flea-bitten bitch stole twenty dollars and a jug of Kentucky whiskey from me, too."

Emory, the sallow-faced man who tended Bisonette's cattle, laughed.

The fifth member of the group, who was visiting from Red Rock, the next station up the road, changed the subject. "Hey, Hicks. You and Jules ever find them horses that was 'missing' from that emigrant train?"

"Sure did," Hicks said. "Got two dollars a horse for doin' it, too."

"Where were they?"

"Up in Cedar Canyon—right where Jules and me hid 'em the night before."

The whole table laughed.

"Sh!" the lumber cutter said, pointing at Tom.

Hicks made a deprecating gesture. "What's he going to do? He's just a little soldier boy."

Tom pretended to study the grain of the cedar table-top, feeling his face redden. At last Bisonette brought his meal on a tin plate. There was baked buffalo hump and gravy, along with fried potatoes, squash, and corn bread.

"Drink?" Bisonette asked.

The two men went through this at every meal. It was the station owner's idea of a joke. "Just coffee," Tom replied. "I'm on duty."

"Maybe he ain't old enough to drink," Hicks suggested, to more laughter from the card players.

Bisonette snickered and got the coffee. Tom dug in. The food was far better than the wretched fare usually found at these roadside houses. Tom felt guilty because his rations were so much better than those of his men, who were condemned to sowbelly and hardtack, along with whatever they could hunt in their bit of free time.

"How is it?" Bisonette asked.

"Excellent," Tom said.

Bisonette beamed. He was proud of his cooking. He kept a vegetable garden behind his house, which he tended like a favorite child.

When Tom finished the meal, he rose and walked to the card table, where Bisonette was watching the poker game. "Mr. Bisonette?"

Bisonette turned. "Yeah, sonny?"

"I have a half-dozen horses that need shoeing." Tom's unit had no farrier, so Bisonette had a contract for that service as well.

Bisonette called over his other shoulder. "Nilsson—you got time to shoe government horses tomorrow?"

The blacksmith looked up from his drink. When not working, he sat by himself and drank all the time, never seeming the worse for wear. He shrugged. "Get 'em here early, in case some emigrants come."

"Anything else?" Bisonette asked. He hooked a thumb in his belt, next to the deerskin pouch that he wore there. Tom often wondered what he kept in the pouch. It wasn't tobacco, because his tobacco was in his shirt pocket.

"Yes," Tom answered. "My men don't have any fresh vegetables. I'm worried about their health, and I'd like to contract for some. I'm entitled to issue government vouchers."

Bisonette shook his head. "Sorry, sonny. I don't sell to the military."

"Why not?"

"Economics. I can get more from the emigrants."

"We're doing a job for you. Surely that counts for something?"

"The only thing that counts for me is money," Bisonette said.

Tom controlled his anger. "All right. I have some money of my own. *I'll* buy the vegetables—at your price. How would that be?"

"I'll give you potatoes and squash at a dollar a pound. Lettuce, too, if you want it."

"A dollar a . . . that's robbery."

Bisonette held out his hands. "Emigrants pay it, and they're glad for the chance. They don't call the Smoky Hill Road 'Starvation Trail' for nothing."

Tom had no choice. "I want onions, too. I've seen them in your garden."

"Those onions are for me alone. I don't sell them to nobody."

"Two dollars a pound."

"I told you—I won't sell them at any price."

"Very well," Tom said. "I'll send my orderly for the rest in the morning. He'll give you the money—honest weights, mind."

Bisonette inclined his head. "Always glad to do business with young gentlemen."

Tom went on. "I also need to start cutting wood for winter quarters. I understand there is a good supply of cedar in a canyon near here?"

"An excellent supply, but you stay away from it."

"That almost sounds like a threat, Mr. Bisonette."

"It is a threat. Anyone takes wood from that canyon, I'll shoot them."

"You can't do that. I represent the government, and that canyon is on government land."

"It's my land. I claimed it. I've taken two thousand logs from that canyon; I sold them to the telegraph company to use as poles. I'll cut the rest of the wood for the railroad when it comes through. No one else is going to take it first."

Tom did his best to remain civil. "You make it difficult to defend you, Mr. Bisonette."

"I didn't ask them to send you here. Me and my boys can defend this ranch just fine by ourselves. We don't need no soldier boys to help us."

Tom thought. He could try and take the wood by force, but he couldn't afford to get in a firefight with the local civilians. That would be sure to set some politician howling, and it would look like hell on his record. Besides, Bisonette and his civilians were better armed than his men—he wasn't sure who would win.

The card players were grinning at Tom in open derision. He said, "I've already been told I can't cut wood along the river. Most of the trees there are already gone, and people are complaining to the government about how unsightly it is. So tell me, just where am I supposed to go—all the way to Big Timbers?"

Bisonette grinned. "You learn quick, sonny."

Tom fumed. He felt humiliated, totally inadequate for the job he was supposed to be doing. He bet Bisonette and his men wouldn't treat Jim Starke this way. "Thank you for the meal," he said formally.

Bisonette nodded. Tom turned and left the building, ignoring the laughter of its inhabitants. Outside, he put on his forage cap.

"Lieutenant!" It was Pemberton, the gangly young telegraph operator, approaching him.

Tom had had enough. "What is it!" he snapped.

The young man halted and took a step backward. Apologetically, he said, "The line's dead again, Lieutenant. There's no current between here and Fort Pierce."

"So take your wagon and fix it," Tom told him.

Pemberton looked terrified. "But what if it's Indians?"

"That's the third time that line's been down in the two weeks I've been here," Tom said, "and God knows how many times before that. What it is, is poor construction work."

He calmed down. Why take out his frustrations on poor Pemberton? "I suppose you want an escort?"

Pemberton nodded.

"I'll have Sergeant Hayward detail two men. You can start in the morning, if that would be convenient. Now, if you'll excuse me, it's time for inspection."

5

"D'ye think Oi've got the scurvy?" Thomas McIlhargy asked.

"Your gums bleeding?" Barnacle Bill Sturdivant replied.

"They are."

"You got scurvy, all right." Barnacle Bill had been a sailor, and he knew about such things.

"Jaysus," McIlhargy said. "That means me teeth are going to fall out."

"Get the Professor to make you new ones," Harry told him. "He'll give you wood ones, just like George Washington. Yours are brown anyway, nobody will know the difference."

The men were in front of the Bean Hotel, which was what they called the cook tent. Eustis "Useless" Peel, to-day's cook, dumped the food on their plates, and they took it behind the tents, where they sat in the grass and ate without enthusiasm.

"I thought all this vinegar they dumped on our food was supposed to prevent scurvy," Shorty Ewing said.

Link said, "Obviously it doesn't work, shit for brains."

Frazer's teeth were as bad as McIlhargy's. "This wouldn't happen if we got fresh vegetables."

"Typical army bullshit," Hunter said. "There's enough vegetables across the road to get us all healthy, but we can't have 'em. At least we got my fish. Now if we could only get somebody who knew how to cook." As part of his light duties, one-handed Hunter went fishing each morning. His day's catch of pickerel was on the men's plates, along with the inevitable fried sowbelly and hardtack.

"It wasn't like this in the war," complained Thomas Moonlight, who, with Barnacle Bill, had come over from the guard tent. The other two guards, O'Meara and Patrick Cuddy, were walking their rounds; they were forced to miss the meal and would have to make it up as best they could. "Back then, the ladies' societies used to send us baskets of food and spare clothes."

"Now they send them to the Indians," Link said.

"That's because we're bad men," Hunter said. "We rape women and kill babies."

Frazer, the ex-officer, said, "We did that in the war, too. It didn't seem to bother anybody then. Hell, General Sherman killed more women and children than Red Cloud and Storm and all these other Indian chiefs put together."

"Maybe that's the secret," Hunter told him. "You have to do your killing on a large scale. Then they call you a hero."

The men washed their tin plates in a tub of cold soapy water that Peel had set in front of the cook tent. Then they went back to their A tents to prepare for inspection. Harry shared a tent with Frazer, O'Meara, and his new bunky, Hezekiah Sanders, who had been on herd guard that day.

Harry and Frazer sat on their cots—made of cottonwood poles nailed together, with blankets laid on top—and began polishing their accoutrements. Kiah, who was ready for inspection, took out his paper and pencil. "Another letter, Kiah?" Harry asked. "I thought you just wrote one?"

Kiah, who had quit a small Methodist college in Ohio to come west, shook his head. "Got a lot to say, I reckon. I'm hopin' to get this one done in time for the next eastbound stage."

Harry shined his brass belt buckle, scrutinizing it from different angles. "Think you'll get one from your girl this time?"

"I better."

"She doesn't seem as gossipy as you are," Frazer remarked.

"Maybe she's got things to do at home," Kiah replied. "Maybe the mail ain't getting through too good from the States."

"Maybe she's got another fellow."

Kiah blanched, and Harry said, "Leave him alone. You're just jealous 'cause no girl would have you."

Frazer went on, heel-balling his carbine sling until it shone. "What do you find to write about, anyway? This place couldn't get any more boring."

"Oh, this and that," Kiah said. "It's like that when you miss somebody."

"If you miss her so much, why'd you join up?"

"Didn't know I was *gonna* miss her. It's the first time Sarah and I have been away from each other, you see. We've known each other all our lives."

"There's the trumpet," Harry said, grabbing his jacket. "Fall out."

They went outside, where Link and Lieutenant Conroy were waiting. At a post this small, Conroy had decided to hold nightly inspections instead of the usual parade. The men had not brought their dress uniforms with them, so they wore garrison uniforms along with their arms and the white gloves they used on guard.

"Squad," Link ordered. "Ten-shun!"

Eight men snapped to.

"Present—arms. Inspection—arms."

Lieutenant Conroy came down the line, with Link a step behind. Conroy checked the men's uniforms and weapons. He paused in front of Shorty Ewing. "Where's your belt, Ewing?"

The little grocer stood at attention, staring straight ahead. "I don't know, sir. I can't find it. It was in the tent this afternoon, I swear it was, but now it's gone."

"You lost it?"

"Yes, sir. I mean, I don't know, sir. I guess so, sir."

Conroy turned. "Sergeant, take this man's name—he's out of uniform. Ewing, your pay will be stopped the cost of the belt, plus you'll pull latrine detail for two weeks."

"Yes, sir," Ewing said, shaken up. He was a conscientious young man who didn't like getting in trouble.

With the inspection concluded, Link dismissed the men and they returned to their tents, where their time would be their own until lights out. Shorty Ewing placed his Spencer carbine in its rack at the end of his tent. He looked around, hands on his hips. "I know I had that belt. What the devil could have happened to it?"

McIlhargy, who had just come in, caught his eye. Nervously, he motioned toward Walsh. The young tough had pushed his forage cap back on his head and was unbuckling his belt. Ewing's eyes widened.

"Hey, that's mine! You stole it!"

Before Walsh could turn, Ewing flew across the tent, landing on Walsh and knocking him to the floor, smashing the bigger man with both fists. "You son of a bitch!"

He grabbed Walsh by the throat, strangling him. McIlhargy yelled. He tried to pull Ewing off, but the little man was too strong. Walsh's face was turning blue. His eyes were popping out of his head.

Link heard the noise and rushed in. "Knock it off!" he shouted. He and McIlhargy tried to loosen Ewing's grip, but they couldn't. Harry, Frazer, and Kiah Sanders came in. With difficulty, the five of them dragged Ewing off Walsh. Even as he was pulled away, Ewing lashed out with his fists at the prostrate Walsh, who was choking and gulping for air.

"That's enough!" Link told Ewing, pushing him across the tent.

"He tried—he tried to kill me," Walsh gasped.

"No great loss," Link said. He turned to Ewing. "What's this all—"

"He stole my belt," Ewing said, still enraged. "I didn't lose it, he took it. Take a look, my initials are on the back."

Link took the belt from the cot and examined the back. A smile crept over his weathered features. "Well, well, what have we here—a barracks thief? Streak, I'm gonna make you wish you'd never—"

At that moment Lieutenant Conroy ducked into the tent, along with one of the guards—Walsh's friend Moonlight. "Ten-shun!" Link ordered.

The men snapped to. "What's going on?" Conroy demanded. He looked at Walsh, who was sitting now, gagging and spitting up phlegm, his face bruised and puffy from Ewing's fists. "What happened to that man?"

Link handed Conroy the belt. "Ewing's belt, sir—the one that was missing. Walsh stole it."

"Is that true?" Conroy asked Walsh.

Link kicked the sitting man. "On your feet when an officer speaks to you." He pulled Walsh upright.

"Did you steal this man's belt?" Conroy repeated.

Walsh looked sullen. "No."

Link smacked him in the ear. "Say 'sir,' you thieving bastard."

"That's enough, Sergeant," Conroy said. "I don't condone physical abuse."

Link let go of Walsh, who said, "I didn't steal it, *sir*. I just borrowed it, like. I was going to give it back."

Conroy didn't believe him. "What happened to *your* belt?"

Walsh stretched his bruised neck. "I give it to an Indian girl. Sir. At the squaw camp."

"You gave it to—you mean, she prostituted herself for a *belt*?"

"Yes, sir." Walsh managed a grin, more confident now. "She'd do it for just about anything, sir."

Conroy pursed his lips. "Theft of a fellow soldier's property is a serious offense, Walsh. I'd put you in the guard tent, but I can't spare the manpower. You're to be fined a month's pay plus the cost of the belt. Stable police and latrine detail until further notice. That's . . . you disapprove, Sergeant?"

He had caught the look on Link's face. Still at attention, Link said, "Barracks thief, sir. I'd have him spread-eagled."

"I said I don't believe in such measures."

"Beg pardon, sir, but stopping a man's pay don't mean much when he don't know when his next pay is coming. Men like this don't understand nothing but force. You got to teach 'em a lesson and teach 'em good."

"The sentence stands, Sergeant."

"Sir, I—"

"Are you arguing with me, Sergeant?"

Link stiffened. "No, sir."

"Very well," the lieutenant said. "Carry on." To Moonlight he said, "You may return to your post."

"Yes, sir."

Conroy left the tent. "Conroy's soft," Frazer remarked when he was gone.

"What he is or ain't is no concern of yours," Link told him. He turned to Walsh. "You're lucky, Streak. I'd have had the hide off you."

Walsh gave Link and the others an insolent grin, then he left the tent, too.

There was a sudden buzz of conversation; everyone wanted to know what had happened. "You should have seen him," McIlhargy told the others. "Fell on poor Walsh like one of them avylanches."

Ewing said. "Why didn't you tell me he'd stolen the belt before?"

The young Irishman looked down. "Oi—Oi was scared of him, Oi guess. Oi didn't know you was going to get in trouble."

Ewing was still angry. "The bastard, I'm—"

Link grabbed his shoulder. "Save it for the Indians, Avalanche. He won't bother you no more."

Link left the tent. The rest of the men returned to their quarters. "You going to put this in your letter?" Harry asked Kiah, " 'Exciting details of army life—the Purloined Belt Recovered.' "

Kiah laughed. The two young men had become good friends. They shared much the same background. Kiah sat on his cot, scribbling away in the rapidly fading light. Harry knew he should write home, too. He'd been neglectful in that line; funny for someone who'd been so homesick when he'd joined up.

Across from him, Frazer lay on his cot with his hands behind his head. "Telegraph's down, I hear."

"Did Indians do it?" Kiah asked. "What do you think, Harry? You've been out here awhile."

Harry was always surprised that anyone considered him a veteran, let alone an expert on Indians. He frowned and tried to look knowing. "Hard to say."

Frazer waved them both off. "There ain't no Indians around here—not hostiles, anyway. What this means is that somebody's going to get the gravy train, going with Pemberton to—"

Outside the tent there was a pistol shot, followed by a cry of pain.

"Now what?" Harry said, and the three men grabbed their carbines and hurried outside.

6

Somebody was groaning on the far side of the tent line, facing the road. Harry, Kiah, and Frazer went through the opening between tents along with the rest of the platoon. The men were in various stages of undress, carrying carbines and pistols.

They saw Tom McIlhargy rolling around in the short grass, holding his bloody shoulder. "Holy Mother," he moaned, "Oi've been shot."

The men hurriedly formed a skirmish line, expecting to find themselves under Indian attack, but there was no attack. The plain was blanketed by the stultifying quiet of a late summer evening.

The men looked around, puzzled. "Was it a sniper?" George Frazer wondered.

"No sniper," Link said, pounding up. "That shot came from these tents."

Lieutenant Conroy was right behind Link, along with the guard—Corporal Anders, Moonlight, and Barnacle Bill, their carbines at port arms. Conroy looked haggard after a long day. "What's going on?" he said. Then he saw McIlhargy. "Good Lord," he breathed.

After ascertaining that there was no immediate danger to his command, Conroy knelt beside the wounded man. "How are you, soldier?"

McIlhargy grimaced, hand pressed against his shoulder, trying to stem the flow of blood through his fingers.

"All roight, sir."

"What happened?"

27

"Don't roightly know, sir. Oi was walking to the latrine, and then Oi found meself on the ground."

From behind them came Hunter's voice. "Ask *him*
what happened."

They turned. With his good hand, Hunter held Useless
Peel by the collar. Peel was a nearsighted fellow, with
strawlike hair that stuck out in all directions. He was the
dirtiest soldier in the company. Hunter shook Peel's collar. "Go on," he ordered. "Tell them."

Conroy stood. Peel's face was a mask of helpless stu-
pidity. "I was in the tent," he said, "cleaning my pistol.
I—I dropped it, and it went off."

"Christ," Link swore, rolling his eyes.

"You idiot!" Conroy kicked at the ground. "What the
hell else can go wrong around here?" He immediately
cursed himself for showing emotion in front of the men.

Some of the men looked and found a bullet hole in the
wall of the tent that was shared by Peel and Hunter,
along with Pennock and Patrick Cuddy. Link knelt beside McIlhargy. "How is he?" Conroy asked.

Gently, Link removed McIlhargy's hand from the
wound. The Irishman winced. "Burns loike hell, so it
does."

Link examined the wound. "He'll be all right, sir. Bullet's got to come out, though. He'll have to see the doc
at Fort Pierce."

Conroy nodded. "We'll put him on the next stage
east." He knelt beside the wounded man again. "Just lay
quiet, son. You'll be fine." Son? he thought. McIlhargy's
only a few years younger than me. To Link, he said,
"What's the usual treatment for an injury like this?"

"With no doctor, sir? Clean the wound with whiskey,
then give him quinine mixed with whiskey every few
hours."

"They issued me quinine with the company supplies.
I can buy whiskey at the station."

"Yes, sir. And sir—get the good stuff. Rye or bourbon.
If that Injun whiskey don't kill him outright, it's liable to

infect the wound. God knows what they put in it. Don't let that French bastard up there trick you."

"All right." Conroy stood. "A couple of you men get him back to his tent."

Link stood as well. "Beg pardon, sir. Mac needs peace and quiet. He won't get that in his tent. Why don't we put him in that abandoned house up the road?" He indicated an old log cabin near the station.

Conroy didn't know. "That would mean detailing a man to keep watch over him, and the duty rosters are stretched thin as it is."

"I'll stay with him tonight, give him his medicine. That way nobody'll have extra duty. He'll be on the stage tomorrow."

"Very well," Conroy said.

Link turned. "Mad Dog, Sanders—bring his cot, we'll use that as a stretcher. Avalanche, get the bandages and that bottle of quinine from the company stores." He squatted beside the wounded man again. "You're going back to the fort, rookie. It's the gravy train for you."

Hunter leaned over and patted McIlhargy's good shoulder cheerfully. "Watch out for Doc Dudley. He kills more men than he cures. If he has to amputate, make sure he takes off the right arm."

Beneath his freckles, McIlhargy turned even paler than he already was.

Harry and Kiah got McIlhargy's cot. With the help of Barnacle Bill Sturdivant, they lifted the wounded man onto it. "That's what you get for rattin' out on me," Walsh told McIlhargy smugly.

"Go to hell, Walsh," McIlhargy said.

Harry and Kiah hoisted the improvised stretcher. As they did, Harry noticed Frazer talking in low tones to Walsh and Moonlight. Those two lowlifes seemed like odd company for the former officer to keep. Then Harry shrugged it off and helped carry the stretcher to the abandoned house.

* * *

Tom Conroy could not sleep. He lay on his cot, staring at the roof of his tent, the white canvas luminescent in the midnight darkness.

Tom was worried about Indians. He was worried about how he would perform if the station was attacked. He had made his preparations. He had assigned defensive positions, and his men knew what they were supposed to do. But would they do it? Or would they panic and do something stupid? These were raw recruits for the most part, not seasoned veterans who could be counted on to do the right thing with a minimum of direction. Most of these men had never seen combat. A great deal of their performance, Tom knew, would depend on his own.

Certainly his performance so far had been nothing to celebrate. His little command was falling apart before his eyes. He felt like everything that had gone wrong had been his fault. If he had done his job better, McIlhargy wouldn't have been shot, Walsh wouldn't have been a thief, Bisonette and his men wouldn't humiliate him and deny him lumber. He should have stayed in New York, like his parents wanted, making the social whirl. He felt like a total failure, and he wondered if he'd gotten in over his head by joining the army. He wasn't officer material. He couldn't command; he couldn't lead men. He couldn't think of a single thing that he'd done right since—

His tent flap opened. "Sir?" It was Corporal of the guard Anders, the ex–Foreign Legionnaire.

Tom sat up. "What is it, Corporal?"

There was a reluctant note in the big Dane's voice. "You had better come, sir. Private Cuddy was just up at the abandoned house, checking on the wounded man. . . ."

"Is McIlhargy all right?"

"He's fine sir. It's Sergeant Hayward. He's . . . he's gone, sir."

Tom swung off the cot. "Deserted?" he asked, even as he knew that was impossible.

"No, sir. I don't think so, sir." Anders wasn't telling him everything. Anders couldn't cover up for his friend Hayward because one of the guards had officially reported Hayward missing. Tom bet that Anders had taken his good time getting here, though.

Tom pulled on his trousers and boots and followed Corporal Anders to the abandoned log cabin. A kerosene lamp burned inside, throwing weak light into the prairie darkness. O'Meara stood beside the open door. He came to attention, presenting arms, as Tom went in.

McIlhargy lay on his cot, his wounded shoulder bandaged, sunk into any uneasy sleep. The bottle of quinine powder sat on the floor beside him. The bottle of whiskey—Jim Beam—was there, too.

The whiskey bottle was empty.

Damn Hayward, Tom swore to himself. He tricked me, set me up like the rawest rookie. "Corporal Anders—call out the guard."

Even at this late hour, Jules Bisonette's stage station roared with life. The poker game was in full swing. There was talking and laughter. Whiskey was passed from cup to cup. Thick wreaths of tobacco smoke mingled with the stale smell of sweat.

Suddenly the noise died and everyone looked toward the open door. Link Hayward stood there, swaying slightly, fists on his hips, one corner of his mouth curled in a grin.

"Where's that asshole that says the army can't fight?"

7

Tom Conroy ran toward the stage station, his new Smith & Wesson revolver in hand. Behind him came Corporal Anders, Moonlight, and Sturdivant, with their carbines. As they neared the station, they heard yelling and oaths and the sounds of furniture being broken.

The soldiers went inside. The buckskinned civilian called Hicks lay sprawled against the bar, bloody and unconscious. Sergeant Hayward was fighting Bisonette and three other men. They went back and forth across the room in a swirl of confusion, pounding with fists and feet, breaking chairs and bottles. Hayward was getting the hell beat out of him.

"Break it up!" Tom cried. "Halt, I said!"

The fight went on, and Tom motioned to Anders. "Give them a volley. Into the roof."

"Ready," Anders said. "Fire."

Three carbines rang as one. The fight stopped. The four civilians turned, some with fists still raised, while Hayward sagged to the floor. Dirt trickled from the ceiling where the bullets had struck. The soldiers levered fresh shells into the chambers of their Spencers and cocked the hammers.

"That's enough," Tom told the civilians.

Jules Bisonette stepped forward, anger clouding his dark face. There was blood on his knuckles and down one side of his cheek; his checked shirt was ripped open. "Well, well, it's the little soldier boy. Take my advice, sonny—don't come onto my property and tell me what to do."

Tom had had enough—enough of these insolent civilians, enough of the army, enough of people taking him for granted. "I *am* telling you what to do. The next volley will be into your midst."

Bisonette was surprised by Tom's vehemence. "You wouldn't," he said.

"Try me," Tom said. Beside him, the three soldiers had their carbines leveled.

Bisonette didn't call him on it. "You think it's all right for your man to come in here and start trouble?"

"Sergeant Hayward will be dealt with according to military law."

"And what about my station, eh? Who is going to pay for the damage? *You?*"

"Frankly, Mr. Bisonette, I wouldn't give a red cent for your station and all the property in it. If you want money, submit a claim to the government. Better yet, gouge the emigrants for it. That seems to be your primary occupation."

Bisonette moved forward. "You're getting pretty big for your britches, sonny. I've a good mind to break you in half."

Tom's grip on the pistol tightened; his thumb pressured the hammer. "That's fine by me, Mr. Bisonette. Let's shoot it out, shall we? Toe to toe, across the room, across the road—I am at your disposal as to distance."

Bisonette hesitated, unsure what to do. Behind him, Emory the cattle herder took a threatening step, until Anders pointed a carbine at his stomach. "Do not think about that, *mon ami.*"

"Well?" Tom demanded.

Bisonette gave in. "Go ahead. Get him out of here. Make sure he doesn't come back."

Conroy stepped toward Hayward. "On your feet, Sergeant. You're under arrest—drunk on duty."

Hayward staggered to his feet, battered and bruised,

his blue jacket torn. He wiped blood from his nose. "Oh, hell, Lieutenant—"

"You will address me as 'sir' or 'Lieutenant Conroy.' You will stand at attention, and you will not use profanity. Is that understood?"

Hayward grinned crookedly. "Sure, Lieutenant—"

"Add insubordination to that charge," Tom said.

"Hey, wait—"

"March him out," Tom told Anders.

Moonlight and Sturdivant took positions on either side of Hayward as Anders barked, "Prisoner, atten—tion! Left—face! Forward—march!"

As the little party started for the door, Hayward waved to the civilians. "So long, boys. I enjoyed the party."

When the enlisted men had gone, Tom pulled a silver dollar from his trousers and tossed it onto the unconscious form of Hicks. "Buy that man a drink."

Tom left the station, catching up to the others. Anders was calling cadence in his heavy accent. "Your left, your left. Your left, right, left."

Tom drew level with the prisoner. "Hayward, you fool, what were you thinking of in there? If we hadn't come when we did, you'd have been killed."

Hayward staggered along, staring straight ahead. He didn't feel much pain now, but he would tomorrow. "It just seemed like the thing to do, sir. Came on me all of a sudden. That bunch gets my craw."

"How long did it take you to drink that bottle of whiskey?"

"About fifteen minutes, sir."

Tom was aghast. "You're lucky you aren't dead."

"I seen it done quicker, sir."

The little party returned to camp. To Anders, Tom said, "Put the prisoner in the guard tent, Corporal. I want him paraded tomorrow for punishment. If he tries to leave, shoot him."

"Yes, sir," Anders said. "Where are you going now, sir?"

"To bed, if it's all right with you. I've had a long day, and I'd like to get some sleep."

8

The next morning, the old guard escorted Link to roll call. He stood at the end of the formation—dirty, uniform torn, face busted to hell. His head throbbed from too much alcohol and from the fists of the civilians at Bisonette's station.

Since Link was under arrest, Corporal Anders took the roll in his place. When Anders had reported all present, Lieutenant Conroy said, "Sergeant Hayward?"

"Sir?"

"You were drunk on duty and insubordinate. As of now, you're reduced to the ranks."

"Yes, sir," Link said without batting an eye. It wasn't the first time this had happened.

Tom hadn't wanted to do this. He couldn't let Hayward get away with the stunt he'd pulled last night, though. If he did, what little semblance of order that remained in his command would be gone. He went on. "Corporal Anders, I'm appointing you acting sergeant."

"Yes, sir."

"Private Frazer—you're acting corporal in Anders's place. You'll be the new corporal of the guard."

Frazer held back a smile. "Yes, sir. Thank you, sir."

Tom neither liked nor trusted Frazer, but he had no choice. He needed a corporal. Of his veterans, Campbell was a shirker, Woodruff would be discharged in less than a month, and Walsh was worthless. That left Winston, and he couldn't justify giving Winston rank—the boy couldn't even march properly. Frazer was a recruit, but he had prior military experience, so he got the job by default.

Tom addressed the formation. "I've tried to treat you people like men, but it hasn't worked. Very well, we'll try the Old Army way of doing things. Sergeant Anders?"

"Sir?"

"Private Hayward is to be taken to the parade ground and spread-eagled."

"Yes, sir. For how long, sir? I believe four hours is the usual sentence."

"Make it six. Private Campbell is to be taken there as well."

Hunter's jaw fell. "What'd I do?"

Anders said, "How long for Campbell, sir?"

"Until he regains the use of his hand."

Hunter gulped. "But sir—I'm a cripple."

"The sun cure is said to work wonders," Tom told him. He went on, "Private Peel—you were neglectful with a government firearm. Plus you've been dirty at every roll call since we've been here. You're to be spread-eagled for four hours, then go on stable police. And if you're dirty tomorrow, you'll go back out in the sun."

Peel was scared; he tried to steady himself.

Anders said, "Anything else, sir? What about the telegraph detail?"

"It can wait till tomorrow. We don't have enough men right now. Who's cook today?"

"I am, sir," Harry said.

"Go to the station and pick up the vegetables I ordered from Mr. Bisonette. And don't overcook them."

"Yes, sir. I'll try not to, sir."

"Don't try—do it," Tom snapped. He nodded to Anders. "You may dismiss the formation, Sergeant."

"Yes, sir."

As Anders got ready to issue his orders, Tom stepped close to Hayward. "Am I doing better, Hayward?"

"Much better, sir. You're having fun now. I'm proud of you."

9

"Ow!" Link said. "Not so tight." Link lay on his back in the center of the parade ground. Skull Anders had extended Link's arms to their fullest, driven two stakes into the ground, and tied Link's wrists to them. Under the guard of Shorty Ewing, Hunter and Useless Peel awaited their turns at the torture.

Skull spread Link's legs as far as they would go before staking them to the hard ground. "Jesus Christ, you French son of a bitch, what are you trying to do—tear my legs off?"

"I am not a French son of a bitch. I am a Dane," Skull said, tying Link's right ankle to the stake.

"I think I liked you better when you were a private."

Skull was unimpressed. "This is nothing, my friend. In the Legion, when I was there, this would be considered the gravy train."

While Link muttered obscenities, Hunter was staked out, then Useless Peel. As Skull finished with Peel's bonds, Frazer, the new corporal of the guard, came by to inspect the prisoners. "Who are these," he said, "the Three Wise Men?"

"Go to hell," Link told him.

Frazer smiled. "Not so big now, are you, Hayward? Well, enjoy your day." He laughed and walked away.

* * *

The sun beat down on the spread-eagled men, searing their uncovered faces. Clouds of flies swarmed over them, biting them. The three men screwed their eyes shut to keep the flies out. They closed their mouths and tried to blow the clustered flies out of their noses. In the heat, it was hard to breathe. Peel panicked and opened his mouth, taking a deep gulp of air. A clot of flies was sucked down his throat as well, and he began choking and coughing.

"I've got to get out of here," he screamed, straining at the rawhide thongs that bound him.

"Shut up," Link told him. "No wonder they call you Useless."

Peel was crying like a baby now, rolling his head from side to side, tears running down his cheeks. His whimpering was the only sound on the parade ground other than the buzzing of the flies.

As the morning wore on, the three men's faces blistered, especially their eyelids, which were unused to the sun. The fiery ball drilled through the thin membranes until they thought their heads would explode. They turned to the side, trying to get their eyes away from the sun, but it didn't help.

"Water," Peel moaned, but no one brought water.

After the flies came the ants. Red fire ants—first the scouts, then columns, swarming around the men, marching up their trouser legs and shirtsleeves. Peel let out an anguished cry that could be heard all over Buffalo Creek Station. "Oh, God, help me! They're eating me alive!"

"Be quiet, stupid," Link said. "Just keep your eyes closed tight so they can't get in there, and you'll be all right."

Peel broke down—blubbering and crying, occasionally screaming, then subsiding into a tearful murmur—while Link and Hunter endured the torture quietly. After four hours, Peel was released to stable police. Frank Walsh and Ewing helped him to his feet. They had to steady him and hold him upright until he regained the use of his limbs. Still crying, he brushed ants out of his clothing and hair, swiping weakly at the flies that continued to feast on him. Finally he staggered off, leaving Link and Hunter.

"Two hours left for me," Link muttered. "At least I'm getting out of this. A cripple like you, you're liable to be here for the rest of your enlistment."

Hunter didn't answer. He was stretched taut, back arched in agony, gritting his teeth and trying not to cry out. His head flopped back and forth and tears came from his eyes.

Link opened his eyes a crack and looked over. "What's wrong?" he asked through the red film of his own pain.

Just then, Harry Winston ambled up, taking a break from his duties at the Bean Hotel. "Hi, boys. Having a good—oh, Jesus." He stopped when he saw the condition the two men were in.

"Mad Dog," Hunter croaked, straining against his bonds. "Mad Dog. My ear. Filled with ants. Get them out. Come on. Christ, hurry, please. They're eating into my brain."

"They won't find much when they get *there*," Harry remarked, kneeling. A stream of red ants tunneled into Hunter's left ear. "Shit," Harry said in revulsion.

Gingerly he dug the ants from Hunter's ear, shaking them off his fingers.

"Hey, you—Winston! Leave that prisoner alone!"

It was Frazer. "Snot-ass," Link muttered. "You can tell he used to be an officer."

Frazer crossed the parade ground. "What are you doing here, Winston?"

Harry got the ants out of Hunter's ear before he stood. "I was crossing the parade ground and my cap blew off," he said.

"Don't give me that shit, Winston. You were trying to help these mill birds. You better watch yourself."

"Fuck you, Frazer. Lighten up. You're not a colonel or general or whatever it was anymore. You're just a jumped-up little corporal."

On the ground, Hunter laughed through his pain. "Listen to Mad Dog," he told Link. "Sounds like he's on his second enlistment already."

Harry started away. Enraged, Frazer was about to go after him when Hunter called out, "Hey, Frazer—come back here."

Tom Conroy watched his fatigue party work on the stables. He had only four men available, but they were getting more done than any group since the platoon had arrived at Buffalo Creek. No one wanted to be the next to be spread-eagled.

The army was crazy, Tom thought. These men were like children. The only thing they understood was brute force. You had to act like a—

Corporal Frazer marched up, snapped to attention, and presented arms. "Sir, one of the prisoners wishes to speak to you. Private Campbell, sir."

"Very well," Tom said. "Carry on," he told the fatigue party. "No slacking off."

Tom accompanied Frazer to the center of the parade ground, where Link and Hunter were staked out under a cloud of flies. Tom's stomach turned at the sight, but he had to pretend to be hard and unmoved.

"What is it, Campbell?"

Hunter looked up at him, making slits of his eyes to protect them from the sun. Hunter's face was blistered, swollen from fly and ant bites, his lips puffed. He spoke through gritted teeth because of the pain. "You won't believe this, sir, but I've got the use of my hand again. It's a miracle, sir. I think all it needs now is for me to get up."

"How much can you use it?" Tom asked.

"Maybe half, sir."

"Not enough." Tom turned away.

"Seventy-five percent?" Hunter suggested.

"You're not leaving here until you receive a full cure."

"All right, all right—I've got full use of it. I told you it was a miracle."

Tom glanced at Frazer. "Cut him loose."

Frazer bent and cut the ropes that bound Hunter to the stakes. "Work that hand," Tom ordered.

Hunter rolled over, moaning with relief.

"Work it!"

Hunter held up his hand. He made a fist, flexing his fingers.

"Amazing recovery," Tom observed. "The Lord works in mysterious ways."

"Yes, sir," Hunter said. "Very mysterious, sir."

Scraping insects from his face and clothes, Hunter slowly rose. He teetered on his feet, then straightened, attempting to come to some form of attention. His head felt as though someone were pounding an anvil inside it.

"Get yourself some water," Tom told him. "Then join the fatigue party at the stables. If there is a recurrence of your injury, you will return here to the 'dispensary' for treatment."

"Yes—" Hunter choked on the flies in his mouth. "Yes, sir. Thank you, sir." He saluted, turned, and walked stiffly away. Then he fainted and fell on his face.

"Carry him to his tent," Tom told Frazer.

Tom looked at Link, still on the ground. Link had been in bad shape before this ordeal started. Tom could only guess the pain that the man was in now, because he never let it show. Tom was tempted to be merciful and let him up, but he restrained himself. That would be viewed as an act of weakness, and these men took advantage of weakness. Besides, in some curious way, he felt that Link would resent his sentence being lessened. He seemed to pride himself in being able to take punishment.

Tom turned away and went back to the stables, leaving Link alone under the broiling sun.

10

The stage from Cheyenne Wells pulled in late that afternoon. Manfred "Dutch" Hartz, the Swiss Bible reader, was in charge of the escort. "Any sign of Indians?" Lieutenant Conroy asked him when he reported in.

The owlish corporal stood at attention, caked with dust from the ride. "No, sir. It was quiet as you could ask."

Tom nodded. "Very well. Dismiss."

Hartz saluted and left, leading his horse.

Two days since the squaw camp pulled out, Tom thought, and no sign of anything unusual. Hayward's hunch must have been wrong. There wasn't going to be Indian trouble. Thank God. Tom had a hard enough time commanding these men in garrison; he didn't know if he could have handled a battle. He took a deep breath and relaxed.

The men were getting ready for dinner when the stage arrived. Harry ran into some of the escort as they came back from the horse lines. "Hey, Professor—heard the news? Link isn't sergeant anymore."

"There's a surprise," cracked Miles Woodruff, the angular dentist known as the Professor. For some reason Woodruff had cut off most his beard, until now it looked like someone had glued a shaving brush to the point of his chin. "What did he do this time?"

"Got drunk and tore up the station. Skull's the sergeant now. Frazer's corporal."

"Frazer?" the Professor said. "That dickhead? I'm glad I'm getting out. I wouldn't want to take orders from him."

"How many days you got left?" Elias Rhinehart asked him.

"Twenty-seven."

"Lucky bastard. You going back to the fort to be discharged, or they going to do it here?"

"Who cares, as long as they discharge me? I've got my money saved. I can't wait to get back to Pennsylvania and start pulling teeth again."

Dutch Hartz came up behind them. "Me, when I am discharged, I am going to invest my savings in one of these new Kansas railroad towns. I believe there is much potential here. You should stay, too, Professor—you have no ties back East. Why don't you think about it?"

The Professor shook his head. "I wouldn't come west of the Mississippi again if you paid me. I like civilization."

"Say, what happened to the squaw camp?" Ike Pennock asked Harry. Ike was a pork packer from Missouri who had joined the army after his business went bust.

"Pulled out," Harry told him. "Just like that."

Dutch frowned. "That is strange," he said, and there was uneasiness in his voice.

"Who's going to do our laundry now?" Ike worried. The Indian women had done the men's washing in return for surplus sowbelly and hardtack.

"Try doing it yourself, asshole," Hunter said from behind them. "Why do you think God put that creek there?"

The men turned and recoiled at the sight of Hunter's sun-blistered, swollen face. Zurawik, the handsome young Pole, crossed himself. "Good God, what happened to you?"

"I got spread-eagled," Hunter told him.

"What for?" the Professor asked.

Hunter held up his formerly paralyzed hand. "This. Boy Wonder turned bad-ass all of a sudden. He got Link and Peel, too. That was right after Peel shot McIlhargy."

"Peel shot . . . ?" Dutch shook his head in disbelief. "You have had a busy few days here, haven't you?"

Not long afterward, the stage from the East arrived. The escort from Fort Pierce, Third Platoon men, got to stay the night at the station and eat there—it was part of the government's contract with Bisonette. After dinner and inspection, they came down to Camp Conroy, where they had a good laugh at Link's demotion and the spread-eagling of the three men that afternoon.

"Bring any whiskey?" Link growled at them.

"No," said their corporal, Zimmerman.

"Got money to buy some?"

"If I did, I'd have bought it for myself by now. There still ain't no word on our pay. Starky's hoping it'll come next month."

"Lou says to tell you hi," another of the men told Link. Lou was a whore who followed Link from post to post, with a daughter that was supposed to be Link's, though he never admitted it.

"It would've been better if she sent a bottle," Link said.

"She tried, but Cronk found it." Cronk was the company first sergeant.

The newcomers *had* brought something from the fort—mail. There was nothing for Harry, but Kiah Sanders got two letters, along with a photograph of his girl, Sarah.

The men crowded around for a look. The sepia-toned photograph showed a well-dressed young woman posed thoughtfully against a dark background. The men whistled. "Whoa, she's a real looker."

Moonlight said, "I'd like to get in her—"

Link rapped him behind the head. "Watch your language, Midnight. That's a respectable lady. She ain't like your mother."

Moonlight flared, but did nothing. The rest of the men settled in for a night of yarning, but Harry rose. "I'm going to bed," he said. "I've got stage escort in the morning."

"Me, too," Link said.

"You got the gravy train, then," Corporal Zimmerman told them.

"Yeah," another of the Third Platoon men agreed. "Nothing ever happens on stage escort."

The men detailed for stage escort were awakened by the guard before dawn. They dressed and ate, then Frazer, Moonlight, and Ewing went for their horses. Harry and Link would be riding in the coach. In part this rotation of men was to save wear on the horses; in part to provide firepower for the coach if it was attacked. The day was already warm as the two men filled their canteens from the creek.

Harry and Link fell in for inspection as the others led their horses from the picket lines. The men wore their field gear. Harry's wide-brimmed hat had once belonged to Steroverovka. His cavalry shell jacket with the cutoff collar had been the Russian's, as well—Harry had bought it when the dead man's effects were auctioned at the fort. A calico bandanna was knotted around Harry's neck. Link wore a battered slouch hat and a shapeless blue jacket, much mended and patched. There were darker spots on the jacket's faded sleeves where noncom's stripes had come and gone over time. George Frazer had fitted a cloth down the back of his forage cap to protect his neck from the sun.

The men stood at attention, carbines hooked to the leather slings over their shoulders. Harry and Link were not required to wear the heavy slings, but the slings were a distinguishing mark of the cavalry, so they were worn as much as possible, despite the discomfort. After Skull inspected the men, Frazer marched them to the station.

The westbound stage was leaving first. Hicks and Emory were leading horses from the corral and putting them into the coach's traces. They saw Link and glowered. Link grinned at them. The eastbound stage's escort loitered by the corral gate, along with wounded McIlhargy, who was going back with them. There was a strong smell of bacon and coffee from the station's open doors.

The stage driver and guard came out, draining their coffee cups and eating doughnuts. They were just a couple of kids. Back East, people had an image of stagecoach drivers as grizzled old-timers, but it required strength and endurance to handle the six-horse teams over difficult terrain and in all weather. Like soldiering, it was a young man's game. While Emory held the near leader, the driver climbed onto the box and the guard opened the door.

"All ready!" the guard cried.

The passengers emerged from the low building. The first was a tall, handsome woman, composed and self-assured, wearing a wine-colored traveling outfit and plumed hat. She was followed by an avuncular, bearded gentlemen carrying a heavy leather satchel. Lastly came a short, bespectacled man in a checked tweed suit, canvas gaiters, and derby hat. They stepped into the coach, followed by Link and Harry, holding their carbines. The guard shut the door and climbed onto the box, while Frazer called out, "Prepare to mount. Mount."

Link and Harry settled onto the leather-covered bench opposite the passengers. Link cast an appraising eye at the woman. Above them there was a whip crack and yells, then the coach bolted forward, groaning on its thoroughbraces, while the mounted escort trotted behind.

11

The stagecoach jolted over the prairie. The rutted road cut across the bends of the river, so there was no tree line to break the endless horizon of sand, sagebrush, and sky. It was fifteen miles to Red Rock Station, where the horses would be changed and the passengers could stretch their legs and ease their battered kidneys. Frazer, Moonlight, and Ewing rode a distance behind the coach, out of the dust.

Inside the coach, Harry Winston felt cut loose from reality, set adrift in an alien world. The only reminder of civilization was the detritus that littered the roadside. There were abandoned wagons, dry-rotting in the sun, along with the bleached skeletons of cattle, horses, and mules. There were discarded trunks and furniture and household items, even a cast-iron stove. Occasionally there was a grave marker, as well, to point out the human cost of Manifest Destiny.

Around Harry there lingered the faint smell of paint and new leather. The stage line had originally belonged to David Butterfield, but it had been bought first by Ben Holliday, then Wells Fargo, which had refurbished the coaches. Harry felt awkward in the presence of the three civilians; it had been a while since he had been with his own kind. Link continued to ogle the tall, dark-haired woman, who stared out the coach window, ignoring not only Link, but the bouncing of the coach and the dust being blown in upon her. The bearded gentleman sat next to her, the satchel nestled between his legs. He wore

a charcoal cutaway coat and a top hat cocked to one side
of his head. The short fellow in tweeds kept staring at
Link, who looked awful after his beating by the civilians
and a day of being spread-eagled. Finally the man could
contain his curiosity no longer. "Excuse me, soldier.
What happened to your face?"

"I was born with it," Link said. "What's your excuse?"

The woman smiled. The bearded gentleman found
Link's reply amusing as well. "We haven't had soldiers
riding in the coach with us before," he said. He was a
competent-looking fellow, heavyset, as though he enjoyed the good life.

"It's our lieutenant's idea," Link told him.

"My name is Zenas John Lowe. Most people call me
Johnny the Deuce."

"Gambler?" Link asked.

"I prefer to think of myself as a professional gentleman. This is Miss Bell."

The tall woman nodded, favoring the soldiers with
bright, intelligent eyes. Link and Harry touched their hat
brims. "Ma'am," Harry said, and they introduced themselves.

Lowe went on. "Miss Bell and I are on our way to
Denver. We're going to open an entertainment palace
there. It's been our dream to have our own business.
We've been saving our money, and now the dream is
about to be realized. We intend to make it the best house
in the city."

"If not the West," Miss Bell said.

Johnny the Deuce laughed. "That's what I like about
you, Annie. You think big."

The man in tweeds and gaiters extended a hand to the
two soldiers. "Stanley Kimball, *New York Herald*."
Kimball's rimless glasses were surmounted by beetling
dark eyebrows and a shock of brushy hair. He exuded an
air of earnest self-importance. "I'm out here to do a se-
ries of stories on the Indian problem. You may have

heard of me—my book and lecture tour on General Sherman's southern campaign were extremely popular."

"I ain't a reader," Link said.

"I've heard of you," Harry said. "My father's a newspaperman, he's talked about you. You called for harsher treatment of the South, didn't you?"

Kimball smiled. "Complete destruction, actually. It's a disgrace that those people have been allowed to resume their lives as if nothing happened. Atlanta should have been just the start. Every city, every town in the South should be razed, the people should be dispossessed, and their property given to freed Negroes. No fate is too harsh for rebels."

Link and Harry exchanged glances. Annie Bell and Johnny the Deuce looked bored, as if they had heard all this before. Harry wondered how many days they had been cooped up in this coach with Kimball.

"What outfit are you boys with?" Kimball asked the soldiers.

Harry replied, "K Company, Fifth Cavalry."

Behind his thick glasses, Kimball's eyes widened with interest. "That's the bunch from Cheyenne Bluff, isn't it? Were either of you boys in that fight?"

"We both were," Harry said, unable to keep a note of pride from his voice. Link looked at Kimball with disdain.

The newspaperman leaned forward. "What luck. Tell me about it."

"Well," Harry began hesitantly. It was hard talking to an outsider about something like Cheyenne Bluff. "The Indians had us surrounded. It was hot and we didn't have much water. A lot of the boys didn't make it back. It was pretty bad, I guess."

"No, no." Kimball waved him off. "I'm not interested in that part. Tell me about the massacre of the Indian village."

"I wouldn't call it a—"

"Did you kill any women or children?"

Harry had been busy trying to control his horse through most of the attack on the village. He couldn't remember if he'd even gotten off a shot. "No, I don't think so."

Kimball turned to Link. "What about you?"

"Maybe," Link said.

"How did that feel? Did you enjoy it?"

"Maybe."

Kimball studied him. "Yes. Yes, I believe you did enjoy it. My God, what kind of men are you?"

"We're no different than anybody else," Harry told him.

Kimball regarded him with eminent superiority. "Of course you're different. Admit it—you're only in the army because you couldn't make it on the outside. The peacetime army is an insult to the nation. It's an insult to our boys who fought so valiantly during the Rebellion."

"Did *you* fight in the war?" asked Johnny the Deuce, who was tired of Kimball's fulminations.

"I decided I could render more service to the Union through my journalistic endeavors," Kimball replied.

"Ever get near a battle, see the killing close up?"

"The workaday business of killing really didn't interest me. I was more concerned with grand strategy. I concentrated on headquarters activities."

"Where it was nice and safe?"

Kimball ignored the jibe. "I'm not reluctant to say that through my efforts more than one incompetent commander was removed, so I contributed my part to the war effort."

"I'm sure we wouldn't have won without you," Johnny said.

"And what did *you* contribute, sir?"

"About a gallon of blood. I got shot to pieces at Second Bull Run." He had deserted before he was returned to duty, but he didn't tell the reporter that.

Kimball went on, basking in his own importance. "As

far as I and many like me are concerned, the peacetime army should be abolished."

"Who'd protect settlers from the Indians, then?" Harry asked him.

"If it weren't for the army, the settlers wouldn't need protecting. The Indians wouldn't fight. They wouldn't have to. You men are the oppressors of those children of nature. They are being ground beneath your boots."

"Oh, for—"

"You don't deny you're embarked on a war of extermination?"

"I don't know what we're embarked on. We just do our duty."

"Stealing Indian lands—is that your *duty*?"

It was Annie Bell's turn to speak up. "Where are you from, Mr. Kimball?" She had a composed, silky voice.

"Massachusetts."

"Did you know that the people of Massachusetts stole Indian lands and exterminated their owners?"

"I had nothing to do with that."

"Of course you didn't. I was just thinking that you might choose to give your own home and property to the Indians. As a way of making amends."

Next to Annie, Johnny the Deuce smiled. But nothing fazed the pompous Kimball. To Harry, he said, "Indians were tortured at Cheyenne Bluff, were they not?"

Harry remembered how Link had scalped a wounded Indian and pitched him screaming off the bluff. "Maybe they were, but you didn't see what the Cheyennes did to Mick Bannon and Squillace."

"Squillace," Link murmured to himself, "*that* was his name. I could only remember him as Squealer. Boy, did he ever live up to that handle."

Harry went on, angry now. "And how about that little girl we rescued from the Indians—little Becky? I don't think she was upset to see us."

Kimball dismissed him. "My understanding is that white captives—if 'captive' is even an appropriate word—rarely wish to leave their Indian families and return to civilization."

"If you'd seen what the Cheyennes did to her white family, you might not—"

"You're wasting your time, Mad Dog." Link spoke to Harry, but he was looking at Kimball. There was a funny grin on Link's face, and Harry went cold because he knew that it wouldn't take a hell of a lot for Link to kill the newspaperman. "You ain't going to change his mind. He's a *journalist*. He's got his story wrote already. He ain't going to let a little thing like the truth get in his way."

Kimball leaned back in his seat. "My story isn't written, but its shape is clear. I know what the Indian 'problem' is. The problem is the army, and believe me, that is what I shall tell the nation."

Sniffing, he went on, "Look at you, you dress like tramps. You have no manners. You're rapists, cowards, scum. How does it feel to be hated by the entire country?"

"It don't bother me," Link said.

"There's smoke ahead," Annie said suddenly, looking out the window. "Isn't that where Red Rock Station should be?"

Everyone crowded to the windows. Ahead of them rose a thick column of black smoke. Before anyone could speak, the coach gave a lurch. There were oaths from the driver's box, followed by the bark of the guard's Henry repeater.

Kimball was thrown into a corner by the coach's sudden movement, his bowler hat and glasses coming awry. "What the—"

"Indians," Link said, unhooking his carbine from its sling. "We're being attacked."

12

Frankie Walsh was on herd guard. The platoon's horse herd was moved to a different location each day for grazing. Today the animals were about a mile west of Buffalo Creek.

Frankie wasn't paying attention to the horses. Against standing orders he had dismounted, ground-hitching his own mount. He sat in the dried grass, making a deck of cards to replace the one that had been taken from him by Lieutenant Conroy. With a knife, he cut rectangles from sheets of folded letter paper that he'd stolen from that college boy Sanders, then penciled in numbers and suits of the deck.

He smiled to himself as he worked. That dumb-ass lieutenant thought he could keep him from playing cards. Well, nobody pushed Frankie around. Frankie was twenty years old, and he'd spent most of it on his own, on the streets of New York. There wasn't a trick he didn't know. One thing for sure, he wasn't going to let any bullshit army get him killed, not at Cheyenne Bluff or anywhere else. He was too smart for that. Fools like Hayward and Winston might laugh at him, but he'd get them back in time. If he hadn't gotten in bad with the boys that ran his old gang, he wouldn't be in the damn army in the first place.

He penciled in the queen of diamonds, held up the card and looked at it. He was proud of his drawing ability. Maybe he should become an—

Behind him, his horse snorted and shuffled uneasily.

Frankie turned and looked around. He didn't see anything. He was alone out here, save for the whisper of the prairie breeze through the grass and a bunch of quail that squawked into the air nearby.

The horse snorted again. Frankie peered more closely. Maybe there was a snake or something. He saw nothing.

Frankie shrugged. Stupid horse. He hated the damn things. He wished he had joined the infantry. He went back to work on his cards. Next was the king of diamonds.

Suddenly he was punched in the back, hard enough to make him grunt and sit straight up. Wide-eyed, he looked down and saw an arrow sticking through the front of his shirt. Blood began gushing from his mouth and nose. He was hit again, and again, the arrows piercing his body with loud thunks. He stared at the arrows, wondering how this had happened, wondering where they had come from. Then, slowly, he toppled over, with his forehead resting on the ground.

Nearby, two painted Cheyennes raised themselves from a fold in the earth and moved toward the white man. As the Indians' knives started their gruesome work, Frankie's paper cards scattered and blew away on the breeze.

Tom Conroy was in his wall tent, bringing the company log up to date, making a list of which men were on what details, when there was a carbine shot from Guard Post Number 1, followed by cries of "Corporal of the guard!" and "Lieutenant Conroy!"

Tom picked up his pistol and charged from the tent in time to see the platoon's horse herd being driven off by a pair of Indians. The thieves were out of rifle range. There was nothing the soldiers could do but watch helplessly and listen to the Indians' triumphant yipping.

"Sergeant Anders!" Tom said. "Mount every spare man. Get civilian horses from the station, get a horse for me as well. We're going to pursue those thieves."

"Yes, sir," the big Dane said. "What if Bisonette don't want to give us the——"

"Take them anyway."

"Yes, sir." Grinning his death's head grin, Anders hurried off with his five-man work detail. He and Tom both knew that the pursuit would be fruitless, but it had to be done.

The Indians' high-pitched cries receded in the distance. It had all happened so fast. Walsh had been on guard over there; what had happened to him? He had never even fired his weapon. As Tom went back in the tent for his forage cap, he wondered if this was the extent of the trouble or just the beginning—if there were just these two Indians or a whole war party lurking nearby. He wondered if the stage to Cheyenne Wells had gotten through.

13

There was a long rise to the coach's left, and the Indians came boiling over that. There were maybe three dozen in all, faces and bodies painted for war, as were their horses. A few wore feathered bonnets, but most let their long hair stream out behind them. They were quiet; they liked to wait until they got close to their victims before yelling.

"Do they mean us harm?" gasped the reporter Kimball.

"No," Link said, "they're soliciting for the Indian Relief Fund."

The stagecoach made a long turn. In the distance Red

Rock Station was burning; the only choice was to head
back to Buffalo Creek. The young driver cracked his
whip over the leaders' ears. The guard fired his Henry
repeater at the oncoming savages. Frazer, Moonlight, and
Ewing closed up on the coach, nervously pulling their
carbines from their saddle sockets.

Inside the coach Link and Harry each took a side, lev-
ering shells into the breeches of their carbines. Across
from Link, Johnny the Deuce reached beneath his coat
and pulled out a .31 caliber pocket revolver. "I wish I'd
brought something heavier," he swore. "Let me use your
pistol, Mr. Hayward."

Link unflapped his holster and passed Johnny his .44.
"I'll take yours," Annie Bell told Harry.

Harry hesitated.

"Give it to me. I know how to use it."

Harry passed her the pistol.

In the box, the driver urged the team on, but they
couldn't outrun the Indians. All they could do was keep
going and hope for a miracle. Some of the Indians began
firing rifles. Bullets smacked into the coach, splintering
the newly painted wood. Kimball dropped to the floor,
cowering beneath the benches.

"Spencers!" Harry said, recognizing the weapon's dis-
tinctive crack. "They're using Spencers! Where did they
get them?"

"From the government, you idiot, where do you
think?" Link replied. "The Indian agents want to make
sure we don't have no unfair advantages over their pets."

Link and Harry began returning fire, bracing themselves against the coach sides and the wooden benches.
The bangs of their carbines were loud in the small coach.
Black powder smoke mingled with the thick dust. It was
almost impossible to aim with the vehicle's bouncing
and jolting. Johnny and Annie fingered their borrowed
pistols, waiting for the Indians to come within range.

From the box above came a cry and a thud.

"Somebody's hit," Johnny the Deuce said.

"Must be the guard," Link said, squeezing off another round. "The Henry's stopped."

Blood ran from a seam in the box's floor down into the coach. It spilled across the leather seat and onto the cowering Kimball's neck. Kimball reached up to wipe the liquid away, saw what it was, and yelped with terror. The back and forth motion of the vehicle splashed the blood around the interior, and soon all the passengers were splattered with it.

Outside, the three mounted soldiers attempted to maintain a rear guard. They fired their carbines as they rode, the stagecoach's dust choking them, bandannas pulled over their mouths. At first they kept the Indians at bay, then the Indians swept around their sides, threatening to cut them off from the coach, forcing them to close up. As the men used up their carbine shells, they jammed the weapons back in their saddle sockets and drew their pistols.

Suddenly Ewing cried out as a bullet shattered his backbone. The little ex-grocer slid from his saddle, trying to hang on to the pommel but unable to do so. As he hit the ground, his foot caught in the stirrup. He was bounced along for a few yards, then fell free, where he was surrounded by Indians.

In the coach Link said, "They got Avalanche."

Frazer and Moonlight made no attempt to go to Ewing's aid. It would have been pointless. They spurred their horses closer to the coach, coming alongside it. Frazer took off his cap and beat it against the near leader's rump, urging the animal on. "Yah!" he yelled. "Yah!" But the team couldn't go any faster. The two mounted troopers drew ahead of the coach and kept going.

"What are they doing?" Harry said.

"Running," Link told him.

Harry fired and hit one of the Indians, saw him throw up his arms, then lost him in the thick dust. Harry's head was pounding from the slamming of the coach and the

gunfire. Across from him, Johnny the Deuce looked un-
ruffled, holding Link's pistol. Annie Bell was worried
but determined. Harry wondered how far it was to Buffalo Creek—too far, probably. They would never make
it.

There was a strangled cry from the driver's box. Harry
saw one of the long reins dragging in the dust outside
the coach. "The driver's hit," he said.

Annie Bell gasped. On the floor Kimball whimpered,
hands over his blood-splattered head. The coach began
veering erratically. Harry was afraid it would topple over.

Link handed his carbine and a handful of ammunition
to Johnny the Deuce. "Here."

Link booted open the stage door. Hooking a foot in
one of the windows, he reached up to the rail, then
hauled himself onto the roof. He crawled along the roof,
holding the rail with one hand, then lowered himself
onto the box alongside the driver. He shoved the driver
aside and gathered the reins in his hands.

Harry shortened his carbine sling so that the weapon
hung straight down behind his back, and he opened the
door on his side of the coach.

"Where are you going?" Annie asked.

"Up top."

Harry held on to one of the leather hand grips and
leaned out. Below him the ground seemed to go by at a
dizzying speed. He looked away, toward the top. This
wasn't going to be as easy as Link had made it seem. A
bullet smashed into the side of the coach beside Harry's
head, startling him so that he almost let go of the hand
grip and fell off. With his free hand he reached up and
grabbed the brass rail that ran around the coach's top. He
took a deep breath, let go of the hand grip and reached
up with his other hand. He lifted his leg and tried to
hook his heel on the window. He didn't make it on the
first try and found himself dangling in space, holding on
by his hands. The coach was bouncing. The seven-pound
carbine at his back was dragging him down. Desperately

he kicked up his foot and wedged it in the window. Pushing with the foot, he heaved himself upward. He teetered on the edge of the rail, then rolled over onto the coach's roof, with the carbine's metal breech gouging his back.

He moved onto his stomach, hauling the carbine around in front of him. Link saw him and cried, "What are you doing here?"

"I came to get a better shot," Harry shouted back.

Harry almost regretted the better view. From up here he could see that there was no way out. The stagecoach horses were slowing, long ribbons of foam at their mouths, eyes distended with fear and exhaustion. The Indians began yelling now, sensing the kill, waving lances and bows, firing rifles and pistols. Below Harry, Johnny the Deuce opened up with Link's carbine. Harry tried to calm himself and get off good shots. He hit one of the Indians, but there were too many and they were drawing closer with each second.

The road curved around a rocky outcrop and over a slight incline. As Link hauled on the reins, the coach tipped over onto two wheels. Harry went sliding across the roof, catching himself at the last moment on the brass rail. Below he heard Kimball yell. Then the coach crashed back down again, rattling Harry's teeth.

"Do you know how to drive one of these things?" Harry shouted at Link.

"No," Link cried, shaking the long reins. "Take my place if you think you can do better."

The lead Indians drew even with the coach. Annie Bell poked Harry's pistol through the window and fired. An Indian toppled backward off his horse. She fired again, picking her targets deliberately.

Link knew he had to slow the Indians down. Another minute and they'd be able to shoot the coach horses. Wrapping the reins around one arm, he took the stage driver and, with difficulty, heaved him over the side of the coach. He pushed the guard over the other side. As he had hoped, the leading Indians stopped and dismounted around the two men.

Behind Link, Harry was reloading his carbine. "Were they dead?" he cried.

"They are now," Link shouted back.

He had bought them maybe five minutes, no more. The Indians who had been in the rear of the pack forged ahead of the others. The stagecoach horses had about played out their string.

Then, ahead, Link saw a distant line of mounted men in blue. His heart soared. The soldiers must have heard the gunfire. If only these horses could hold on a little longer.

Behind Link, Harry kept shooting at the oncoming Indians, turning from one side of the coach to the other. Inside, Johnny the Deuce was firing as well, his face smeared with dust and powder smoke, the unbuttoned collar of his shirt grimy. A ball plowed into his right armpit and he groaned. He let go of the carbine and began firing Link's revolver with his left hand.

On the other side of the bench Annie Bell fired Harry's .44 until the hammer clicked on an empty chamber. There was no time to reload the cap and ball. She drew a pocket revolver from her sleeve and shot at an Indian riding by the coach. She thought she hit him but couldn't be sure. Small caliber weapons made little impression unless used at point-blank range.

Link urged the flagging coach horses toward the oncoming blue line, swearing at them as if he could propel them by profanity alone. Some of the Indians drew ahead of him. One fired a rifle at the near leader. The horse kept running for a moment, then stumbled and went down. The off wheeler went down at almost the same moment. The team tangled up and the coach piled into them, flipping over twice and crashing down on its side.

Link and Harry jumped clear as the coach crashed. Both lay stunned for a second. Link was up first, reach-

ing for his revolver until he remembered that he'd given
it to the gambler, Lowe. An Indian rode at him with his
rifle lowered. Link somehow managed to throw himself
aside as the weapon discharged; he felt the powder
grains bite into his face. Confident, the Indian jumped
from his horse and came at Link with a war axe. Link
whipped the carbine sling from his shoulder and swung
it, catching the Indian alongside the head with the heavy
metal clip. Before the Indian could recover, Link swung
again and again, knocking the Indian down, beating him
with the clip until his head was a pulpy mess.

Harry scrambled for his Spencer carbine, which had
fallen a few yards from him. All around was dust and
noise. He picked up the weapon, then fell on his back
and fired up at a figure on horseback going by. The Indian pitched off his horse into the dust. He got to his feet
and Harry fired again, putting him down for good.

The stagecoach lay on its side. The horses were
screaming and kicking in a tangled welter of bones and
blood. The coach door was pushed open from the inside,
and Johnny the Deuce emerged, hatless and bloody. He
fired Link's pistol at the milling Indians.

From behind the coach came a volley of carbine fire.
Lieutenant Conroy had dismounted a six-man skirmish
line, Frazer and Moonlight among them, to cover the
stage and its occupants—these men couldn't hit anything
from horseback. The skirmish line moved forward, firing
steadily, and the Indians retreated out of range, yelling
and shooting back at the white men.

Harry and Link ran toward the coach. They assisted
Johnny the Deuce out, careful of his wound. Johnny
turned and helped them pull out Annie Bell. Annie had
lost her plumed hat, but she still had the small caliber
pistol, as well as Harry's weapon. Last came Stanley
Kimball, frantically trying to straighten his glasses,
which had been knocked askew in the crash. Link and
Harry unceremoniously heaved him over the doorsill

onto the ground. Link reached into the coach and retrieved his carbine.

"Hurry!" Lieutenant Conroy cried, advancing with the
skirmish line. Behind the line, O'Meara and Useless Peel
held the horses—even at this distance Harry noticed they
were not army mounts. Bullets and arrows flew around
the whites, kicking up dust at their feet as they ran toward the line of soldiers.

The stage passengers reached the skirmish line, which
halted out of range of the Indians. "Our horse herd was
run off," Skull told Link. "We were chasing them when
we heard your guns."

"Lucky for you, huh?" Hunter added, grinning.

"Where is the stage driver?" Lieutenant Conroy asked.

"Dead, sir," Link said without batting an eye. "The
guard, too."

Harry looked at Link and said nothing.

While Link and Harry gulped water from their canteens, Lieutenant Conroy attended Annie, who was disheveled and splashed with blood. "Are you all right,
ma'am?"

"I've had worse rides," Annie replied coolly.

Suddenly Johnny the Deuce swore and began running
back toward the stagecoach, which was still in range of
the Indian rifles. "What the . . . ?" Hunter said.

"Get back here!" Conroy cried. "What are you
doing?"

Annie must have known what Johnny was up to, because she started back for the coach, too, but Skull
grabbed her arm. "No," he told her. She struggled in the
big Dane's grasp, but he held firm. "Sorry, ma'am."

Link ran after the wounded gambler. Johnny reached
the wrecked coach and crawled inside. As Link came up,
Johnny stood again, holding his heavy leather satchel.

"You came back for your luggage?" Link cried. "Are
you—"

He was drowned out by gunshots as the Indians began
firing at them. Splinters flew from the coach's sides, one

of them digging a bloody furrow in Link's arm. He swore viciously and pushed Johnny back toward the line of soldiers.

"Are you mad?" Lieutenant Conroy asked as they returned. "What the devil's in that bag that was worth risking your life?"

"Nothing," Johnny said, grimacing from the bullet in his side. "Items of sentimental value."

"It must be some sentiment," Conroy remarked.

As Annie came up to tend the bearded gambler, Conroy turned to Link. "You men did good work, bringing in that stage."

"Thank you, sir," Link replied. "Why don't you ask General Frazer here and Midnight why they yellowed out on us?"

"We didn't yellow out," Frazer said from his place in the skirmish line. "We went for help."

"They'd have heard the gunfire without you," Link said.

"That remains to be seen. I was in charge, it was my decision to make."

"And I say you decided to yellow out."

Frazer pointed a finger. "Watch it, mill bird, or—"

"Save it for another time," Conroy told them. "Right now, we've got to—"

"Christ," the Professor said from down the line.

They all turned. In the distance there was a loud rumbling. It made the ground shake beneath them. Across the river more Indians appeared, as if conjured out of the ground.

"There must be hundreds of them," breathed Hunter.

"Holy shit," Link said.

With his elbow, Harry dug Link's shoulder, indicating Annie, who stood nearby. "Watch your language. There's a lady present."

Link grinned at him. "That's no lady, you jughead. She's a whore."

Harry's mouth fell open. Before he could say anything, Lieutenant Conroy cried, "All right, men. Let's get back to the station."

14

Across the river, the Indians sat their horses, watching, waiting, silhouetted against the wide blue sky. The thirty or so Indians on this side of the river, the ones who had attacked the stage, were quiet as well. The only sounds came from the injured stagecoach horses, whose agonized screams were almost human.

"Maybe we could talk to the Indians," Kimball, the reporter, suggested. "Reason with them."

"Good idea," Tom Conroy told him. "You do it. The rest of us are leaving." He went on. "Five us will have to ride double." He turned to Annie. He had overheard Hayward's remark about her, and he was a bit flustered. "You'll take my horse, of course, ma'am—er, miss." He wasn't sure how one addressed a prostitute.

"Thank you," said the dark-haired woman in her silky voice. She returned Harry's pistol to him, then lifted the heavy satchel from the hand of her wounded companion, Johnny the Deuce. "Let me take this."

Tom held the horse's bridle while Annie mounted, riding astride. Skull said, "You'd best have my horse, sir."

"No," Tom said, "I'll ride double like everyone else."

"That wouldn't be right, sir. It wouldn't be proper, not with you an officer." Tom hesitated, and Skull said, "Trust me, sir."

"Very well," Tom said. He felt like a fool now, like a

show-off who had in some way taken advantage of his new sergeant.

Johnny the Deuce was assisted into O'Meara's saddle. Skull paired Kimball with Useless Peel and himself with Barnacle Bill Sturdivant. Harry doubled up with the Professor, Link with Hunter. "Walsh is dead," Hunter told Link while they waited to mount.

"Boo hoo," Link said.

"Injuns got him on herd guard."

"Saves us the trouble."

"Wish we could do something about them wounded horses," Ike Pennock said. "Do we have to leave them like that, sir?"

"Yes," Tom replied. It was too much of a risk for anyone to go back and put the animals down. Besides, the bullets might be needed later. Tom tried to ignore the horses' terrible cries. Their continued agony was his responsibility. War was a hell of a thing.

"All right, men," he said, trying his best to keep cool. "By the numbers, like nothing is happening. Prepare to mount. Mount."

The men swung onto their horses. Those riding double climbed behind their mates.

"By twos," Tom commanded. "At the walk. Forward—march."

The little column started off. The Indians continued watching them.

"At the trot—march."

"Why are they just sitting there?" Pennock wondered.

"Their leaders are making medicine," Link explained. "Letting the spirits tell them what to do."

"I hope the spirits tell them to leave us alone," Barnacle Bill Sturdivant said.

The men were bunching up, their fear communicated to their horses.

"Eyes front," Tom ordered, riding to one side. "Easy, now. Keep your intervals. We don't want to provoke them. Indians are natural hunters. They'll chase anything

that runs from them. Every minute we put them off gives
us that much more chance of getting to the station." He
eased up beside Johnny the Deuce and O'Meara. "How
are you making out, Mr. Lowe?"

"Fine, Lieutenant," the gambler replied. Annie had
bandaged his side with strips torn from his shirt, which
were now red with blood. "It's not the first time I've
been shot. It probably won't be the last."

"Don't you worry, sir," said O'Meara, who had been
an actor in Dublin. "I've got good hold of him."

Harry Winston rode with his hands locked around the
Professor's waist. His wits were clearing enough for him
to realize how lucky he'd been to survive so far. He
could easily have been killed in the stage crash, yet he
hadn't even gotten any broken bones. One elbow of his
shell jacket was ripped open, along with both knees of
his trousers. His field uniform was going to look as bad
as Link's before his hitch was up.

The little party had gone about a mile when there was
a rumbling behind them. The large body of Indians was
crossing the river, joining the others.

"Keep moving," Conroy ordered.

The Indians followed the column, keeping to its left.
There was a long line of them, in single file. Now and
then the sun glared off metal breast or head ornaments or
off rifle barrels.

"Hey," Hunter said, "look at that one—there in front
on the white horse, with the red shield. You know who
that is, don't you? It's our old friend, Storm."

"Thought he was on the reservation," the Professor
said.

"You ain't authorized to think," Link told him. "It's
against regulations."

"Eyes front," Conroy reminded them. "Keep those intervals. Gently, now. Don't move until they do. Peel—
control that animal."

The Indians continued to follow the column, silently,
eerily. Tom calculated the distance to the station. A cou-

ple of miles now—he could see the distant line of trees that marked Buffalo Creek. There was the rise from which he had surveyed the prairie. He grew hopeful. Maybe the Indians would let them get to the station safely. Maybe this was just some kind of—

The Indians put their horses into a gallop.

"Let's go!" Tom shouted.

The little group of whites raced toward the station with the Indians in pursuit, less than a mile behind and gaining quickly. Those riding double quickly fell behind. Tom stayed back with them, drawing his pistol.

Some of the Indians began firing rifles. The range was great, but there was always a chance of hitting something. From ahead Tom heard the report of an army carbine, and he knew that the camp guard had been alerted.

They headed for the ford, bullets whizzing around their ears. Annie Bell rode at the front, the satchel in one hand. Kimball clung to Peel for dear life; his eyes were half shut—it looked like he was praying. The Indians were closer now, with Storm's red war shield conspicuous among the leaders.

They reached the tree-lined creek and galloped down the slope to the ford, splashing across in a halo of spray. Tom went last, pausing to fire his pistol at the oncoming Indians. That slowed them for a second. Then Tom turned and followed the others.

There was frantic movement around the station; horses were being led into the corral. Corporal Hartz had the guard lined up on the west side of the army camp. As the Indians came up from the ford, the guard fired a volley. One of the Indians fell from his horse. The white-gloved guards fired again, then Tom was level with them. "Get to the station!" he ordered Hartz.

Firing as they went, the guards retreated. When the Indians kept coming, the guards turned and ran. Elias Rhinehart, a former printer's devil, was the slowest. Storm caught up to him. At the last moment Rhinehart turned. Both men fired at the same time. Rhinehart was momentarily blinded by the sun's glare, and his bullet grazed Storm's neck. Storm's bullet hit Rhinehart in the chest, knocking him on his back. Other Indians shot bullets or arrows into the fallen soldier as they rode by.

With his last two bullets, Tom provided cover as the guards ducked into the station house. Already shots were coming from inside. Then Tom spurred through the corral gate and jumped from his horse. He helped Skull and Link push the gate shut, dropping the bar into place as the first Indians drove their horses against it.

15

There was a flurry of gunshots as both sides fired point-blank through the picket-log gate. Splinters flew. A bullet clipped Conroy's havelock cap cover. "Shit," Barnacle Bill Sturdivant said, and he sat down heavily with a bullet in his gut. There was a groan of pain on the gate's other side, and something fell against the logs. Horses cried and stamped the gate with their hooves.

Then the Indians backed off. They began riding in a circle around the station, firing rifles and bows. Flushed with the excitement of battle, Tom calmed himself and thought about what to do next. The corral was filled with excited horses. Some of his men, the veterans, were taking places along the corral's perimeter. Others, the new men, stood around waiting to be told what to do.

Sergeant Anders beat Tom to the orders. "Frazer, Moonlight," he cried, "in the stables. O'Meara, you go between the stables and the smithy. Come on, you candy-asses, look alive! Peel and Pennock—get Barnacle

Bill inside, then take the corner of the garden. Find Dutch and tell him to take the wall by the kitchen, him and Cuddy. Zurawik and Sanders can fill in along the south wall. There's enough civilians inside to cover the front." Anders was calm. He'd been under fire dozens of times. He probably enjoyed it, Tom thought.

"Right, Sarge," one of the men cried as they all ran to their positions. Somebody was already firing from inside the smithy—it must be the reclusive blacksmith, Nilsson. Harry and the Professor had taken places at the corral's southeast corner, where two unbroken lines of picket logs came together. Hunter and Link were nearby, along the east wall. They fired through loopholes in the unusually well-joined wall, ignoring the bullets and arrows that came at them. Harry was ravaged by thirst, but there was no time to drink. He was sore and so tired that if he stopped for a moment, he was afraid he'd fall asleep.

"I knew it!" the Professor roared, firing his carbine. "Twenty-six days till my discharge, and the army's going to get me killed. Typical army bullshit."

Harry's carbine was empty and he turned away to reload, pushing shells into the butt tube. As he did, an arrow chunked into the cedar log where his head had just been. "I thought Kimball said we had exterminated these people," he cried.

"For once, I wish that bastard was right," Link shouted back.

The station was enveloped in dust and powder smoke and yelling. Now and then one of the attackers or their horses fell. One of the Indians stopped his horse outside the stable. He climbed from the horse's back onto the stable roof and moved across, hoping to get a good shot. Inside the stable, Frazer and Moonlight saw a trail of dirt falling from the sod roof. They both fired upward at the same time. Outside, O'Meara fired as well. The Indian spun around, fell on the roof and lay still.

Tom Conroy broke open his Smith & Wesson and reloaded. Sergeant Anders was walking the perimeter, encouraging the men, telling them to take their time. He seemed to have matters well in hand, so Tom went in the station house.

The low-ceilinged house was thick with powder smoke. Chairs and tables were knocked over. There were cards and chips scattered on the floor. Liquor bottles had been smashed by stray bullets. Sturdivant was propped in a corner, with Annie Bell tending him. Hicks and the so-called lumber cutter were firing through loopholes in the shuttered windows. Johnny the Deuce, bandage red with blood, was shooting a pistol through the partially opened door, leaning against the jamb for support.

Kimball crouched under the long table, coughing from the smoke. "Get yourself a weapon," Tom told him.

"No," the reporter replied, looking up through his thick glasses. "As a U.S. citizen, I demand protection from these savages. You have to—"

"Oh, shut up," Tom said.

At that moment the lumber cutter fell back from the window with the top of his head shot away. Annie Bell stepped over the mess, grabbed the dead man's Henry repeater, and began firing out the window in his place.

Tom went out the back door, crossed the gateway, and entered Bisonette's house. The house consisted of one room divided by an oilcloth partition. Bisonette and Pemberton the telegrapher were there, with piles of shell casings at their feet.

"Are all your people accounted for?" Tom shouted above the gunfire.

Bisonette didn't look up. "All except Emory. He was out with the cattle."

Across the road Tom saw Indians swarming around the telegraph relay station. "They've left the wires alone so far," he observed, puzzled. "Usually the first thing they do is cut them down. Unless they knew that the wires were down already."

He looked at Pemberton. "They must have cut the line

the day before yesterday. Your repair party would have been riding into a trap."

Pemberton paled. He looked ill.

Tom couldn't help but smile. "There's one bit of luck that's come out of this—eh, Mr. Pemberton?"

The boy gulped.

Tom grew serious. "The fort will think the line's down because of another accident. It will be days before they send help."

"These Injuns won't be around that long," Bisonette assured him. "Hit and run, that's their style."

Bisonette backed away from the window to reload. Tom took his place, firing his pistol. "You know Indians," Tom said. "What tribe are these?"

"Northern Cheyenne, by what I can see of their markings. Dog Soldiers. Arapahoes, too. Mebbe even some Sioux—I hear there's Sioux hostiles runnin' with the Cheyennes now."

As the station owner returned to the window, the Indians withdrew out of range, taking their dead and wounded with them, leaning down from their horses and picking up the bodies with spectacular displays of horsemanship.

"Cease fire," Tom told the two civilians. "Conserve your ammunition."

He stepped to the back door to repeat the order to his men, but again Sergeant Anders was ahead of him. His loud cry of "Cease firing!" reverberated through the station.

Somebody in the station house was still shooting. Tom went back in there. Hicks, the station's buckskinned second in charge, was firing through the shuttered window. With a gloved hand, Tom pulled his rifle barrel down. "I said, cease firing."

Hicks glared at him. "Don't tell me what to do, soldier boy."

"I can, and I am."

"Since when?"

"Since right now."

Bisonette came in. "What's the matter?"

"Tell this tin soldier who runs this station," Hicks said.

"I've done that," Bisonette replied. "More than once."

Tom said, "Things have changed, Mr. Bisonette. The army is in charge here now. If I have any problems with you or your men, I'll place you under arrest."

Bisonette hesitated, then said to Hicks, "Ah, go on, Joe. Go along with him—for now." To Tom he said, "This ain't over, sonny. I resent your high-handed attitude. Not only that, but I intend to sue the government for the property damage I've suffered because of your—"

There was a fresh burst of yelling from up the road. Tom stepped to the open doorway. The Indians were looting the army camp, rifling the tents, pulling them over, busting up the wagons. Not far away something pale was lying beside the road. It was Rhinehart, or what was left of him after he had been stripped and mutilated. Tom wished they could bring in the boy's body, but it was impossible. There was more yelling downriver, where another bunch of Indians was stampeding Bisonette's cattle, shooting rifles and pistols into the animals as they went, for sport.

"They must have got Emory," Bisonette said.

"Damn," Hicks swore. "That bastard owed me money."

"Let 'em have their fun," Bisonette went on. "The sooner they're done, the sooner they'll leave."

A bullet splintered the door next to Tom, making him jump back. "Something tells me they may stick around awhile," he said.

16

Across the road, the Indians had occupied the two houses and the telegraph office, and from these positions they began sniping at the station. Another Indian positioned himself on top of the blacksmith Nilsson's house, opposite the west wall and the stables. The Indians couldn't see over the picket fence, so their fire was more of an annoyance than anything else, though an early shot struck one of the horses running loose in the corral. The horse screamed and sunk to its knees.

"Pennock, Moonlight, O'Meara," Skull cried. "Get the rest of those animals in the stables, where they'll be safe."

While the three men led the horses into the adobe stables, the other soldiers greedily quenched their thirst, draining their canteens. Many knocked off their hats, letting the breeze cool their sweaty hair. Link removed his carbine sling and his bloodstained jacket. He pulled his buck knife from his belt. Gritting his teeth, he cut open his red flannel shirt and undershirt, then dug the jagged stagecoach splinter out of his left arm, just above the bicep.

"Jeez," Hunter winced, next to him, "why don't you let the Professor do that?"

"The Professor's a dentist," Link replied. "That Injun shot me. He didn't bite me."

Then the splinter was out—it was a good two inches long. "You could build a fire with that," Hunter cracked. Link looked at the splinter, then tossed it away.

Lieutenant Conroy and Skull walked the corral's perimeter. Still bothered by the old wound in his hip, the big Dane hobbled along, carbine in hand, sweat pouring from his close-cropped blond hair. "Clean your weapons," he told the men. "Those Spencers will jam if they get dirty."

The two men stopped at Link's position. Link, Hunter, Harry, and the Professor rose to their feet and came to attention, ignoring a sniper's bullet that kicked up dust nearby.

"At ease," Tom told them. "Hayward, what's your assessment of what these Indians will do next?" He felt funny asking advice of a private, even one who used to be a sergeant, but Hayward had been on the frontier longer than any of them.

Link ran a hand through his dark, curly hair. "Well, sir, I know it's strange for Injuns, but it looks to me like they're settling in for a siege."

"And in that case—what?"

"Hard to say, sir. Try to keep us awake all night, would be my guess, then jump us at first light."

Tom nodded. "Very well. As you were."

Tom and Skull kept walking. "There's food in Bisonette's storehouse and water in the well," Tom told his new sergeant, "so we're in good shape there. It's ammunition I'm worried about." The men had started the day with the standard field issue of a hundred rounds per carbine and twenty-four per pistol, though Hartz's guards might have been able to grab more when he lined them up.

"God knows what they have left," Tom said. "The Indians got the rest of our ammunition when they captured our camp. Bisonette won't have ammunition for the Spencers, but he should have some for the revolvers. Redistribute the carbine ammunition, make sure every man has an equal amount. Then go in the storehouse—break it open if you have to—and get as much pistol ammunition as you can."

"Yes, sir," Skull said.

"I don't want any man firing unless the order is given, or he has a sure target."

"Yes, sir."

"Have a detail fill all the buckets they can find with water and carry them into the station house. There's a body in there"—Tom never had learned the lumber cutter's name—"have it taken out and buried in the garden. I want this place squared away."

"Yes, sir," Skull said again. The two men completed their rounds and went into the station house.

Inside the station house the civilians had temporarily relaxed. Johnny the Deuce sank to the floor, his bearded face drained with pain and fatigue. Annie Bell knelt beside him. "How are you?" she asked.

He shrugged. "This messes up our plans, doesn't it?"

"No, it doesn't. I won't let anything stand in the way of my dream, and neither will you."

He patted her shoulder. "Good girl. Where's my bag?"

"Right over there. I'll get it for you. I'll get you some water from the well, too."

Nearby, Hicks was reloading his Henry repeater. When he had satisfied himself that another attack was not imminent, he waved aside some of the powder smoke that clogged the room. "Damn," he said, "fighting Injuns works up a thirst. I need me a drink." He went to the bar, found a bottle that hadn't been smashed—the place reeked of liquor—and poured whiskey into a tin cup.

"Good idea," Bisonette said. The station owner got a bottle and cup as well. Then he picked up a second cup. Leering at Annie, who had just come back with the well water, he said, "How 'bout I buy you a drink, missy?"

Annie looked at him coolly. "I think not."

"Oh, come on," Bisonette laughed, "I won't bite you—not right away I won't, anyhow."

"No, thank you."

Bisonette reddened. "What's wrong—you think you're too high-toned to drink with me?"

"Something like that," Annie said.

At that moment Tom and Skull entered. Tom stopped as he saw what was going on. Liquor and a woman could make for an explosive situation, he knew, especially with several hundred hostile Indians outside. He thought of his men, and of what would happen if they got hold of the liquor.

"The bar is closed," he announced.

"Go to hell," Bisonette said, pouring more whiskey. It's my bar. I can drink, or buy my friends a drink"—he winked at Annie—"anytime I want."

Tom stared at him for a moment, then turned. "Sergeant Anders, get three reliable men and destroy all the liquor in this establishment."

Skull gave his lieutenant a shocked look.

"You heard the order, Sergeant. Carry it out."

Skull gulped. "Yes, sir." He gazed at the whiskey bottles like a father who had just been ordered to kill his children. Then he went to the door. "Dutch! Professor! Sanders! In here, on the double!"

Enraged, Bisonette came over to Tom. "You can't do this."

Tom ignored him as the three men Skull had called came in. "The lieutenant wants this liquor destroyed," Skull told them.

"All of it?" Dutch asked, wide-eyed.

"That's right," Tom said. "Keep the rest of the men away from it, too—especially Hayward and Campbell. Search the storehouse for more when you're done."

"Yes, sir," the Swiss corporal said, grinning at Skull's discomfort. He looked at his two men. "We'll be doing the Lord's work today, I think."

The detail took the bottles from Bisonette and Hicks. Hicks started to resist. "Don't try it," Skull told him with his carbine cradled in his arms. Hartz and his men brought their weapons to the ready.

Hicks and Bisonette were outgunned; they had no choice. Growling, Hicks gave up the bottle. Then the detail started on the bottles remaining behind the bar, hauling them out back, uncorking them in a corner of the corral and pouring the contents onto the ground. Tom heard cries of protest from the men outside.

"God damn army," Bisonette swore. "You're worthless as tits on a bull. That liquor is my livelihood. What if the Indians turn around and go now? Where does that leave me?"

Tom said, "I'm sorry, Mr. Bisonette, but I can't take that chance."

"You upstart pup, I'll have your commission. Wait and see if I don't."

Tom went over to Kimball, who was sitting in a chair by the table, trying to calm his jittery nerves. Tom said, "You, whoever you are . . ."

The reporter stood, holding out a hand. "Stanley Kimball, *New York Herald.*" He ducked involuntarily as a sniper's bullet thunked into a window shutter.

Tom didn't take the hand. "Well, Mr. Kimball, make yourself useful and clean up that mess." He pointed to the floor and the gore from the lumber cutter's head.

Kimball looked at the mixed brains and blood, and he paled. "You're not serious."

"Quite serious."

"You've got a woman here. Let her do it."

"The woman fought. You didn't."

"You can't make me clean it up."

"If you want food or water while you're here, you will."

"But I—I don't know how to clean up something like that."

"Learn," Tom said.

Outside in the corral, Link and Hunter butchered the horse that had been wounded and that Hunter had subsequently killed with his knife. Harry and Ike Pennock

readied a fire nearby, while O'Meara searched the storehouse for frying grease. Some of the other men had
gathered around, looking alternately at the horse and at
Hartz's detail, who were now carrying kegs of whiskey
from the storehouse, broaching them with their carbine
butts and letting the red liquid drain into the sand.

"Look at all that beautiful whiskey," Moonlight said,
groaning. "It could be doin' some fellows good."

"It's a sin," Pennock said. "A damn sin."

O'Meara sighed. "Sure, lads, and don't I wish I was
an earthworm over there."

"Skull ain't even trying to save none for us," Hunter
complained. "What the hell's wrong with him? Those
stripes must have went to his head."

"No use worrying about it now," Link told them, wiping his bloody hands on his trouser legs.

"You're taking this well," Hunter said as he hacked
another steak from the horse's flank.

"That's 'cause an army travels on its stomach, and
right now I'm thinking about dinner. This is going to be
the best meal we had in weeks. We just need something
to go with it." His eyes turned toward Bisonette's garden, and a smile creased his leathery face.

Inside, Tom crouched beside Sturdivant. The ex-
sailor's wound had been bandaged by Annie, and he was
in pain. "You're gut-shot," Tom told him. "I can't give
you water."

Sturdivant nodded, understanding. His canteen lay by
his side. Tom removed the wounded man's bandanna and
wet it. "Suck on this, maybe it'll help. We'll get you to
a doctor as soon as we can. You, too, Mr. Lowe."

The gambler nodded, watching the Indians through a
crack in the door. The heavy satchel was by his side. The
telegrapher Pemberton had come into the station house,
as well. He was scared of being left alone next door. Behind them Zurawik, the young Pole, and Peel carried the
lumber cutter's body outside, while Kimball attempted to

clean the floor. It looked like the first time he'd ever had to clean anything in his life. Bisonette and Hicks talked together in low, angry tones.

Tom rose. He couldn't put off this next part any longer. He walked over to Annie, who was leaning against the long table, seemingly lost in thought. "Miss Bell?"

The dark-haired beauty straightened. "Yes?" she said, smiling and revealing strong, even teeth.

Tom clasped his hands behind his back and tried to look stern. "I understand that by profession you are a . . . a . . ."

Her smile faded. "A soiled dove? A frail sister? Fallen angel? *Nymphe du pave?* Why don't you just say what you mean, and call me a whore?"

Tom cleared his throat. Annie didn't look like a prostitute, but he wasn't sure what a prostitute looked like, not in the daylight anyway. He tried to picture her in low-cut red satin and gaudy jewelry, in some luridly lit hell like those he'd visited in his Yale days, but it was hard. He had never thought of these women as having lives on the outside.

"What you call yourself is your concern. My concern is your profession and its affects on my men. I must warn you to keep away from them."

She looked at him contemptuously. "Your men couldn't afford me."

From behind the bar Bisonette spoke up. "I can afford you, missy. I got plenty of money—gold, too, not army greenbacks. What say you and me go over to my house for a while? Your fancy man's in no shape to pleasure you just now."

"I got money, too," Hicks chimed in. "Let's all go."

"That's enough," Tom said. Angrily he turned to Annie. "I repeat—you will not ply your trade at this station while there is a military emergency. You will keep away from the men as much as possible. Having you here is a decided inconvenience."

"What would you like me to do?" she said acidly. "Go outside and give myself to the Indians?"

"Hell, no," Hicks shouted. "Make 'em pay, like everybody else."

Hicks and Bisonette laughed. Johnny the Deuce watched the two men coldly. Then Bisonette's expression changed as he smelled food being prepared. He charged out the back door and looked at his once beautiful garden, which was now a landscape of holes and turned-up dirt.

"My onions!" he shouted at the soldiers. "You bastards stole my onions! Nobody eats them but me!"

Tom came up behind him. "War is hell, isn't it, Mr. Bisonette?"

The station master rounded on him. "All right. You had your fun. You proved what a big man you are. But let me warn you, sonny. Don't turn your back on me. You might find a bullet in it."

17

During a lull in the action, Skull reorganized the men around the station's rectangular perimeter, putting them back into their squads and groups of four as much as possible. He set a guard rotation, including the civilians, so that one man was always on watch along each wall.

Next, Skull inspected the men's weapons, making Peel reclean both his carbine and pistol. After that Lieutenant Conroy called a formation. "At ease," Tom told the men when they had lined up. "Men, we need a volunteer to ride to Fort Pierce for help. I'll level with you, it's a dangerous job. You'll have to go right through the Indians. But there's no choice. There's not many of us, and we're low on ammunition. We can't hold out for long. You'll leave after dark. If you ride all night, you should reach the fort early tomorrow. With luck, a relief column can be here by tomorrow evening. Now, who'll go?"

Link's hand shot up.

"Sorry, Hayward. I need you here."

Link groaned with disgust. Harry and Zurawik raised their hands. Harry was volunteering partly because he wanted to, partly because he still felt a need to prove something to Link and the other veterans.

Tom thought for a moment. "I'd like to send you, Winston, but you're not that good a rider."

"Please, sir," Zurawik said. "In Poland, I was in cavalry."

"That's no recommendation," Link complained. "I mean, who have the Poles beaten lately? Come on, sir, let me do it."

"No," Tom said. There were no other volunteers. "All right, Zurawik, the job's yours. Pick one of the civilian horses, then get yourself some rest."

The young Pole grinned and slapped his chest. "You see, now I get to be hero. Hero in America."

"Just watch out you don't get dead," Hunter told him.

"That's all," Tom told the men. "Dismissed."

The men had full stomachs after their meal of horse-meat and onions. Some of those who were off duty fell asleep. Others congregated at the well, next to the kitchen, to refill their canteens and those of their bunkies. As Ike Pennock lowered his and Hunter's canteens into the well, he turned to Peel, who was next in line. "Why couldn't you'd have shot me instead of McIlhargy? At least he's out of this."

Peel grinned stupidly, revealing broken, yellow-brown teeth with what looked like black tar between them.

Next to him, the Professor recoiled in horror. "Peel, I

could buy a house off what it would cost to get your mouth fixed."

"Well, I ain't gettin' it fixed," Peel retorted, "so you can forget the house."

At that moment a sniper's bullet hit the kitchen wall and everybody ducked. As they got up again, Link sauntered by. "Where are you going?" the Professor asked him.

"Pittsburgh," Link said.

"You're going to the station house, aren't you? To try and scrounge some booze. Well, you won't find any. Me, Dutch and Kiah—we got it all."

"Think so?" Link replied confidently. "I bet there's one place you didn't look."

"Where?"

Link smiled, shaking his head. He went inside. It was cooler in the house, though it still smelled of gunpowder and spilled whiskey. Other off-duty men were there as well. The card game had resumed at one of the tables, with Johnny the Deuce playing draw poker against Bisonette, Hicks, and Kimball. The young telegrapher Pemberton was on watch at one of the windows, looking this way and that. Sturdivant was propped in a corner, moaning and gritting his teeth against the pain of his stomach wound.

The blacksmith, Nilsson, sat alone in one corner, as always. "Why'd them soldiers have to take all the whiskey?" he grumbled, staring at his big hands folded on the table. "What are we supposed to drink?"

"Try water," Link suggested.

"I don't want water. I want whiskey." There was a note of pathetic desperation in the blacksmith's voice.

Outside, the sniping had grown heavier. Bullets thudded into the building's sod walls with increasing frequency. "They're wasting a lot of ammunition," observed Patrick Cuddy, the New York farm boy.

"They've got a lot of it to waste," said Frazer, who

lounged against the wall, watching the card game. "They got it from us."

"Why don't you do something?" Kimball snapped at Lieutenant Conroy. "You're the army, that's your job. We wouldn't be in this mess if it wasn't for your misguided policies. It's not right that innocent civilians should be subjected to this. It's intolerable, in fact. I have a schedule to keep. I have deadlines to meet. How am I going to get my work done?"

"Just make it up," Tom told him. "That's what you newspaper people usually do, I believe."

Behind his rimless glasses Kimball grew angry. "I intend to give your name prominent mention in my story, Mr. Conroy—and it won't be in a flattering light, either. You're a prime example of the kind of officer the army sends out here—arrogant and pigheaded. Not like the fine young men we had during the war, not like them at all."

"Hey, Four Eyes—you in or ain't you?" interrupted Bisonette from across the table. "The raise is twenty dollars."

Kimball looked at his cards again. "I'm afraid I must fold," he said at last.

Bisonette shoved the pipe back in his mouth. "That's twenty to you, Hicks."

Hicks tossed two double eagles onto the pot.

"Lowe?" Bisonette said.

The wounded gambler pushed some coins forward. "Your twenty, and raise you fifty."

"Fifty?" Hicks said. "Damn, that's too rich for my blood. I'm out."

Bisonette wasn't backing down. "Fifty," he said, "and fifty more."

"Let's make it interesting, shall we?" Lowe said. "I'll raise a hundred."

"I thought this was a friendly game," Bisonette said.

"Maybe I'm not your friend," Lowe replied. "Maybe I take offense at your remarks to Miss Bell. Because of my wound, I'm unable to challenge you physically, so I'll do it this way. The raise is one hundred. What do you say?"

Bisonette rose and went behind the bar. He pulled out a cigar box, brought it back, and plopped it on the table, opening the lid. "There's four hundred dollars in here, more or less. All the cash I have right now. Will you risk that much?"

Everyone in the station house was gathered around the table now. Even Pemberton had moved away from his station at the window to watch. Annie had just come back from the kitchen with a pot of coffee. She said, "Johnny . . . ?"

"It's all right," the gambler replied. He reached into his cutaway coat, which hung on the chair behind him, and pulled out a billfold. He counted out four hundred dollars in greenbacks and laid them on the table.

"Greenbacks ain't worth as much as gold out here," Bisonette said, eyes alight.

Johnny took out fifty dollars more and added it to his pile. "Good enough?"

Bisonette nodded.

"Then I call."

Bisonette put down his pipe. One at a time he turned over his cards—a king, a nine, another nine, a jack, and a jack. "Two pair," he announced triumphantly. "Jacks high."

Lowe turned over his hand all at once. "Two pair— kings high."

Bisonette shot from his chair, knocking it over, his hand going to his pistol. "Why, you—"

Lowe stared at him coolly. "I'm unarmed."

"You bastard, you cheated."

"You got in over your head, you mean."

Bisonette's hand was still on the pistol grip. "I've never lost with jacks—never."

Lowe raked in his winnings, wincing from the strain the movement put on his wounded side. "Then you

should know there's a first time for everything." He
looked at Annie. "I believe I'll have some of that coffee
now, Annie."

He rose stiffly and started for the bar, where the cof-
feepot sat. At that moment a sniper's bullet came
through Pemberton's open window, striking Lowe in the
chest, smashing his clavicle. The gambler dropped to the
floor.

At first no one realized he'd been shot; they thought
he had tripped. Then Annie cried "Johnny!" and hurried
to him. The others huddled around. Tom Conroy ran
over and slammed the window shutter closed.

Shaken, Pemberton looked at the fallen gambler.
"That would have been me, if I hadn't moved," he whispered.

Tom ignored him. "Move aside," he told the men who
crowded around Lowe. "Give him some air."

Annie knelt beside Lowe, holding his head in her lap.
He looked up at her and grinned weakly. "This *really*
messes up our plans, doesn't it?"

"No. No, it doesn't," she assured him. "You'll be all
right."

He coughed blood and shook his head. "The only
place I'm going to be is six feet under. I've bought it this
time."

"Oh, Johnny."

He took her hand. "You'll—you'll do fine, Annie.
You always have."

"But—"

"No buts—understand? We always knew this could
happen. I just never—" he coughed again. "—never figured it would happen like this. That was a thousand-to-
one shot—it seems fitting I guess. I wish . . . I wish I
had bet on it."

Annie bit her lip, tears in her eyes.

One person was not paying attention to Johnny the
Deuce. Link Hayward took advantage of the distraction
to grab the gambler's heavy leather satchel, which sat at

the foot of the poker table. He figured a big-time gambler like Johnny would carry a bottle with him, maybe two—probably good stuff, too. He planned to nick the booze and be out the back door before anyone noticed. He unbuckled the satchel's straps and looked inside.

"Holy shit!" he blurted. "It's full of money!"

18

The satchel was stuffed with greenbacks, stacked and tied in neat bundles.

"Put that down!" Annie cried, frustrated because she couldn't get up without dropping Lowe to the floor.

The other men in the room forgot about the wounded gambler and crowded around Link. "Let me see," said Cuddy. Hicks, Frazer, and Moonlight jostled each other to see who could get their hands in the satchel first.

"As you were!" Tom ordered.

The men stopped. They stood aside. Tom moved toward Link and held out a hand. Regretfully, Link gave him the satchel. Tom looked inside, raising his eyebrows at the sight, then turned to Annie and Johnny the Deuce. "How much?"

"Fifty thousand," Johnny said. "The money to start our new business. Half is Annie's, half—" He coughed, and blood splashed over his beard. "—mine."

"Well, it's ours now." Frazer laughed.

Tom looked at him.

"Spoils of war," Frazer explained. After a second he added, "Sir."

"We're not here to loot civilians, Corporal."

"But Lieutenant, he's going to—"

"Legally, or as I interpret the law, all of this money will then belong to Miss Bell." Tom spoke the words distastefully. "I will assume custody of it until the current emergency has ended and westbound travel resumes."

Several of the soldiers groaned. Bisonette and Hicks exchanged glances. Link scratched his jaw thoughtfully.

Gently, Annie lay Johnny Lowe on the floor and stood. "Perhaps I don't agree with your decision, Lieutenant. As you say—it *is* my money."

Tom said, "I must insist, Miss Bell. It would be too disruptive to leave such a sum with you."

"Why, are you afraid I'll use it to debauch your men?"

"Perhaps."

"How do I know you won't take it for yourself?"

"You'll have to trust me."

"And if I don't?"

"I'm sorry, but you have no choice."

On the floor, Johnny the Deuce beckoned. "Lieutenant?"

Tom knelt beside him. The gambler was fading fast; his voice was a whisper. "Look out for her, will you? Don't let anything happen to her."

"Sure." Tom nodded and stood again. This was the last thing he needed. Holding a fortune for a woman he couldn't stand. Annie Bell had been nothing but trouble since he'd laid eyes on her, and she promised nothing but more trouble to come. Already he felt the men's eyes on the leather satchel. These men would kill each other trying to get hold of that money, even if the Indians were coming through the front door while they were doing it. Tom would have to keep it close to him at all times.

Link and Patrick Cuddy picked up Johnny the Deuce and laid him to rest beside Sturdivant. The gambler's bare chest and the front of his trousers were soaked with blood. Link gave him water from one of the buckets that Tom had ordered brought in. "Sorry, pal," Link said.

Johnny shrugged, his eyes half closed. "Luck of the draw," he murmured.

Across the room Jules Bisonette sidled up beside Annie. In a low voice he said, "Sorry about your man, missy."

"I'm sure you are," she said.

"You'll be needing somebody to take care of you now. I'd be happy to oblige."

She turned and looked him in the eye. "I can take care of myself, thank you."

She started to go, but he blocked her way. "Stay here. I can make you happy, I promise."

"You can make *me* happy—or my money?"

"I don't want the money. I'm just interested in you."

"Somehow I doubt that."

"You shouldn't. You're a fine-looking woman."

Annie said nothing.

"Think about it," Bisonette told her, taking her arm.

"I don't have to." She pulled away. "Now, if you'll excuse me, I have to make more bandages." She went to sit beside Johnny.

Tom took the satchel and moved to the station-house door. He blamed himself for Johnny the Deuce's wound. He should have noticed that open window shutter. He should have done something about it. He had been remiss in his duty, and now he had a man's life on his hands. How many more lives would follow before this was over? Tom wished he didn't have this responsibility. He envied men like Winston and Hayward, men with no worries but for their own safety. He had wanted to be an officer, though, and there was more to being an officer than nicer uniforms and better quarters. Responsibility came with rank, and there was no running away from it—or from its consequences.

He cracked open the front door and peered out. Here and there were dead or wounded horses. The Indians had recovered all of their comrades' bodies except the one on the stable roof. Farther down the road was Camp Conroy, with the tents and wagons overturned, bits of clothing and equipment scattered about, and a few Indians picking through what remained.

The station was surrounded by small groups of mounted Indians, watching and waiting. The main body of Indians seemed to be having a conference down by the river. Tom could see many ponies grazing there. He wondered what they were talking about.

Tom had seen enough Indian fighting to know that ordinarily they would have left by now. This situation was becoming eerily reminiscent of Cheyenne Bluff, and he wondered whether the change in the Indians' tactics had anything to do with Chief Storm's presence among them.

Then he sighed. There was nothing he could do but wait and see what the Indians were up to.

19

Sliding Down Hill was worried.

Sliding Down Hill was a Northern Cheyenne, a noted warrior even though he was quite young. His face was painted red, with black and yellow stripes. In his hair was a single eagle feather, worn horizontally to signify courage. A silver chain was tied to his scalp lock. On his hornpipe breastplate was a whistle made from a bird's wing bone, the badge of the Dog Soldier society. Next to the whistle was a small human figure made of deerskin, topped with the long hair of a buffalo. In battle, this charm became Sliding Down Hill. He could not be hurt unless the charm was hit. The charm had protected him for years; it had protected him again today, when he had been in the forefront of the attacks on the stagecoach and on the white man's camp.

Sliding Down Hill had gotten his name while on his first war party, in his fourteenth summer. With the younger members of the party, he had been left to guard the horses, while the older men had attacked a camp of Crows. In the meantime a large party of Crows had discovered the guards. In the fight that followed, Badger— that had been his name then—was knocked down the side of a cliff. To everyone's amazement, he survived the terrible fall, and all saw that as an omen.

Now, Sliding Down Hill sat in a council circle in a tree-shaded area near the river, along with the war chiefs and great men of the raiding party. It was an honor for one so young to be invited to join the circle. All the famous chiefs and warriors were there—Tall Bull and War Bonnet of the Dog Soldiers, Yellow Bear of the Arapahoes, Gall the Sioux, and many more. The party's leader was a Southern Cheyenne, a Kit Fox soldier of the Hair Rope People named Man Alone. He had formerly been called Storm, but after the last surviving member of his family had been killed by white soldiers, he had left his people and come to live with the Northern Cheyennes. He kept to himself and was regarded as mystical by many of the others, who were secretly afraid of him— and of his powers.

The pipe was passed around the great circle, and each of the leaders, starting with the eldest, rose and spoke his views about what the party should do next. Most favored withdrawing and moving to Big Timbers or to Ash Hollow near the river the white men called Platte. Then Man Alone rose. He was impressive, with a massive chest, prominent nose, and face filled with character. His upper arms and body were painted with the black of the Kit Foxes. He had changed his face paint from the old days. Now his face was black, with red eyes and mouth and zigzagging red lines leading from their corners. There was an eagle feather bonnet on his head and a Lancaster rifle in the crook of his arm.

"My friends," he began, "I have heard talk this day of war in the manner that our wars have always been fought. It is good talk, and well thought, and there was a time when I would have agreed with it. Like you, I know war and love it—the taking of horses and scalps and the counting of coups against one's enemies brings glory and honor and wealth. But that is the old way of war, and the old way will not work against the enemy we face now—the white man. The white man fights only to kill, and if the People are to survive, we must fight that way as well. We must forget honor and coups. We must try to kill as many whites as we can, when and where we find them. Only then will the whites respect us enough to leave us alone or to make a genuine peace. I say that we should begin this new form of warfare here, at this white man's camp. I say that we should remain at this place until all of the whites are dead."

This speech caused a stir in the council circle and among those gathered around it to listen. One after another the great men stood to debate Man Alone's proposal. Some were for it, some against, and some unsure. At last it was Sliding Down Hill's turn.

The young Cheyenne rose slowly, with dignity, like the war chief he would one day be. In his arms was a repeating rifle like the ones the white soldiers carried; strapped to his hip was a pistol. Beneath the war paint, his broad, flat face glistened with sweat. He kept his speech short, as befit his years. "My brothers," he began, "I have listened to what Man Alone has said. My thoughts are these. The old ways of war have served our people from the beginning of memory. Why should we abandon them? Why should we change because of an inferior race? We have made a succesful raid. The soldiers' pony herd has been taken. Scalps have been taken. We have done enough. Let us go from this place and celebrate our triumph. After that we may plan another raid or return to our lodges and prepare for the autumn hunt."

He sat, and Man Alone rose again. Man Alone was determined to impose his will on this council. In the ruins of the soldier lodges he had found a blue soldier cap with the device of crossed long knives and *5/K* on its peak. Man Alone knew that device. These were the same soldiers who had killed his son White Wolf. Heammawihio, the Creator, had sent him great fortune, delivering his enemies to him, and he vowed to take advantage of it. "I say that my young friend is wrong. There has been no triumph. We have taken a few horses, but the white soldiers have many horses. We have taken a few scalps, but the white men are as numerous as the fleas on a buffalo's back, or as the geese that darken the autumn skies. What is the loss of a few men to them? They care nothing for it. They are not like us. Only if we kill many of them will they respect us."

Sliding Down Hill stood again. "Will not killing more of them make them want to kill more of us?"

Man Alone seemed glad of the question. "They already intend to kill us all. They intend to make the earth as if the People were never part of it."

There was much shaking of heads at this—it was a concept these men had a hard time understanding.

Man Alone went on. "It is true that we run a risk by undertaking a war of death, but we run a greater risk by following the old ways. For then we face the certainty not only of our own deaths, but those of our families, and of their families to come. I speak as one who has lost every member of his family to the white man's treachery. Unless we change our way of fighting, there will be no more buffalo to hunt in autumn. There will be no more horses running free. There will be no more People. There will be only the white man. You may say that many of us will die in this new way of war. I say that you are right, but I know this—only by following my road do we have any hope of defeating these savages.

And if we do not defeat them, we are doomed. If we must die, let it be for a purpose."

Man Alone sat. Sliding Down Hill did not entirely trust Man Alone—the great chief was both a Hair Rope and a Kit Fox, and the Kit Foxes thought themselves superior to all other men. Sliding Down Hill suspected that Man Alone was interested as much in revenge for his family as he was in defeating the white men. He wished that this problem of the whites did not have to be argued. He wished that the whites had never been created, or that they would simply go away. He was old enough to remember a time when the white men had been but a marginal presence in the People's lives. Every year they had become more and more of an irritant; every year they had come more and more to dominate the People's thoughts and plans. Sliding Down Hill was unsure what to do about the whites. He only wanted things to be the way they used to be, and he was afraid that was never going to happen.

Now the speakers rose again, to decide on a final course of action, arguing until a consensus was reached. Sliding Down Hill did not need to listen. He already knew what the answer would be. Save for himself and a few others, the members of the council had all been moved by Man Alone's arguments.

They would stay at this place until all the white men were dead.

20

"Hang on, Johnny," Annie Bell said. "Please, hang on."

It was just after dark. The wounded gambler had stopped talking sometime before, though he still acknowledged Annie with his eyes. His breathing had grown shallow and raspy, like the sound of coarse sandpaper on wood. His bandages were soggy with blood.

Annie sat between Johnny and Barnacle Bill Sturdivant. The two men had been placed on pallets of fresh straw from the stables and covered with blankets from the storehouse—Bisonette had objected to the wounded men using the blankets and getting them bloody, because he wouldn't be able to sell them to the Indians later.

Sturdivant was feverish. Annie bathed his face and chest with a wet cloth, and moistened his lips. Then she changed his bandage with strips of calico trading cloth from the storehouse—Bisonette hadn't been happy about them using the cloth, either.

"Why do they call you Barnacle Bill?" she asked as she gently tied one of the strips.

"I was a sailor," Bill replied.

"The navy?"

He shook his head, eyes half shut by the pain, sweat streaming down his face. His breath came in short bursts. "Whaling ship. I made two voyages to the Caribbean and the coast of South America."

94

She gave him a look. "What made you join the army?"

"Wanted to complete my education. I figured that . . . that after a hitch in the army, I'd know everything I needed to make my way in the world." He coughed and grinned weakly. "I didn't count on this."

"How old are you?" she asked.

"Twenty."

Her fingers fumbled as she finished the bandage. Twenty—so young to die. She smoothed back his sweaty hair and smiled at him. She turned to change Johnny the Deuce's bandage, then stopped.

The gambler's bearded head lolled to one side. His eyes stared sightlessly at the ceiling.

Annie's heart froze. She felt Johnny's pulse, then she hung her head. "Oh, Johnny."

The reporter Kimball had been watching. "Is he dead?"

Annie nodded wearily.

Kimball turned to Tom Conroy, who was across the table from him, eating a supper of canned beans. "Happy, Lieutenant?" Kimball sneered. "Here's another name for your butcher's bill."

Tom ignored him. He rose and started for the dead man. Then he remembered the satchel full of money and went back for it. He saw Hicks staring at it as he picked it up. He hated having to go everywhere with the heavy satchel. He felt like a banker carrying it around, or like a lawyer—like his father—but there was no alternative.

Tom knelt beside Johnny the Deuce and made sure he was dead. Examining the body gave him a funny feeling, but he hid it. He was in charge and he was supposed to be unaffected by such things. Annie still sat with her head down. Tom didn't know what to say to her; he didn't know how to express condolences to a prostitute. They weren't supposed to have feelings, after all. "I'm sorry," he said at last, as if the words were forced out of him.

"Yeah," she said without looking up. "So am I."

Tom rose. "Do you want any of his effects? I'm afraid we have to bury him right away."

Annie removed the dead man's watch from his coat, which lay beside him. She tucked the watch into her blouse, then rose, nodding to Tom to indicate that she was finished.

Brusquely, Tom called out the back door. "Sergeant Anders!"

A moment later Skull appeared.

"Mr. Lowe is dead," Tom told him. "Detail four men and bury him in the garden, next to the other one."

"Yes, sir."

While Tom waited for the burial detail, Annie stood by herself. Bisonette moved beside her. "You're alone now, missy. Alone for sure. You'll be needin' that man I spoke about—the same way he's needin' you."

"Go to hell," she told him.

The station owner just grinned.

Skull came back with the Professor, Hunter, O'Meara, and Moonlight. Skull closed the dead man's eyes while O'Meara tied his hands and feet together. Then the Professor and Hunter bundled him into a blanket and carried him outside.

Annie followed. She watched the four soldiers dig a hurried grave by torchlight. Nearby, a shallow mound showed where the lumber cutter had been buried earlier. There were still occasional sniper shots, but everyone in the compound was used to them by now. They barely heard them anymore, unless a bullet happened to strike nearby.

Tom stood beside Annie, shifting the heavy satchel to his other hand. The breeze flapped the havelock cloth of his forage cap. He cleared his throat. "Corporal Hartz is religious. Would you like me to have him read a few words from the Bible?"

Annie shook her head. "That wouldn't mean much to Johnny. He wasn't big on praying, or on anybody praying for him. Maybe he had religion in his way, I don't know. I've seen him give money to help a struggling preacher, but he always did it in a way that the preacher never knew."

She watched as the Professor and Hunter laid the blanket-wrapped body in the shallow grave. "At least he's getting out while he's still on top." She looked at Tom, explaining, "Johnny was always afraid that he'd lose it one day—lose the ability to win, the ability that made him what he was. He was terrified that he might die in poverty. I think it was the only thing that ever really scared him."

The four soldiers began shoveling dirt into the grave. "We'll give him a proper burial, with a coffin, when this is over," Tom told Annie. He almost added, "If we survive," but stopped himself. As officer in charge, he was supposed to exude confidence.

Skull interrupted, touching his hat brim. "Sir? It's time for Zurawik to leave. Before the moon comes up."

"Yes," Tom said. "Thank you, Sergeant. Extinguish those torches when the grave's finished." He started for the stables without excusing himself to Annie. He knew it was rude, but she made him feel uncomfortable, and he was glad for the chance to get away from her.

There was a small group of men by the stables as Zurawik led his horse out. He had picked a chestnut mare with a white blaze—which he had darkened with charcoal. The mare was about seven, heavily muscled, probably not much on flat-out speed, but full of bottom for a night of hard riding. The animal's hooves had been wrapped with buffalo hide to deaden their noise. Everything that was not necessary had been eliminated from Zurawik's McClellan saddle, including his canteen—he could drink from the river. Everything else that could make noise had been tied down.

Still holding the satchel, Tom inspected the horse, then the rider. The young Pole wore a dark shirt, and he had blackened his face and hands with charcoal. He carried his carbine and pistol, along with a knife stuck in the top of his troop boot. There were two spare revolver cylinders in his shirt—there would be no time to reload in a running fight.

Tom nodded approval. "The Indians appear to be concentrated across the road, and to the west and east of the station," he told Zurawik. "There don't seem to be as many to the south. Walk your horse to the river. Keep to the shadows, and get across the river as soon as you can. Once you're clear, mount up and ride for all you're worth till you reach Fort Pierce. Kill the horse if you have to."

"Yes, sir," Zurawik said. The young man seemed calm, capable, ready.

"My compliments to Captain Hayes. Make sure he understands that we're low on ammunition, and how essential it is that help gets here tomorrow. Here's a note for Captain Hayes, and another for Lieutenant Starke if that one doesn't work."

Zurawik tucked the notes in his shirt pocket.

"Very well," Tom said, and he held out his hand. "Good luck."

Zurawik took the hand. "Thank you, sir." Then he grinned; he couldn't help himself. The rest of the off-duty men gathered around, wishing him luck in low tones.

True to the fortresslike nature of the station, a sally port had been built in the south wall, facing the river, just wide enough for a man and horse to squeeze through. The port had been cut from the finished fence in such a way that it was only visible from the outside if someone looked very closely. Tom, Skull, and others walked Zurawik to the gate. Quietly, Link lifted the bar. He cracked open the gate, then he, Skull, and Hunter—who had finished with the grave—slipped through, carbines in hand. The three men fanned out in front of the gate. They took positions and waited a few minutes, listening, straining their eyes into the darkness.

Silently, Link came back. He motioned Zurawik forward. He swung the small gate open carefully, so that it did not creak on its leather hinges. Zurawik and the horse squeezed through. The faint scrapings of the animal's hooves faded, and there was only darkness.

21

The moon rose. Buffalo Creek Station fell quiet except for the occasional bang of a sniper's rifle. Indian campfires flickered around the station on three sides, but no noise came from them.

In the station house, Useless Peel slept unconcernedly, his carbine on the floor beside him. In the stables, Hunter slept as well, dreaming of liquor and women. Beside him, Ike Pennock was unable to sleep, or even to close his eyes, so worried was he about what the next day would bring. By the south wall, the Professor boiled coffee over a small fire, while his bunky Patrick Cuddy fried their iron rations of hardtack and salt pork. Next to them, Dutch Hartz read his pocket Bible by the weak moonlight. Dutch couldn't see the letters, but he knew the words nearly by heart, and the feel of the Holy Book in his hands comforted him.

From the east wall rose the mournful tones of a mouth organ playing "Lorena."

"Stephen Foster?" Kiah Sanders said. "Why don't you play something Irish?"

O'Meara stopped. "Foster's all the rage in Dublin. They're fascinated by anything American over there."

Harry Winston sat with his back against the wall and

his hat tilted over his eyes. "Will you go back to the stage when your enlistment's up?" he asked O'Meara.

The Irishman shrugged. "If I can get the parts, I will. My forte is comedy, you know—Shakespearean or modern, I perform both with equal aplomb. I just had a bloody bad run of luck when I got to America—I gave new meaning to the term 'starving actor.' I actually enlisted out of desperation for a meal. I thought I might find the experience ennobling—'We few, we band of brothers,' and all that—but reality has been a shock. 'We band of drunken clowns' would be more appropriate. Now I eagerly await my exit from this unwanted role of Miles Gloriosus and a return to parts more suited to my abilities." He ran his fingers through his thinning hair. "I'm worried that I may eventually have to wear a wig, though."

"Mr. Lo may save you that trouble," Harry said.

"Aye, there's that to consider."

O'Meara resumed playing his mouth organ. On Harry's other side Kiah was scribbling on a piece of paper. He had finally taken off his white gloves from guard duty that morning, but his once spotless garrison uniform was filthy and powder-blackened.

"Still writing home?" Harry asked him.

"Still writing," Kiah said.

"Who to?"

"My girl."

"How can you even see in this light?"

"Oh, I get by. Got a lot to say before . . . before tomorrow. A lot to say." Kiah paused his pencil. "Say, Harry, will you do me a favor?"

"Sure."

"If I don't . . . you know . . . will you promise to visit Sarah—my girl? Tell her I was a good soldier. Tell her I loved her."

"Christ, Kiah, nothing's going to happen to you. These Indians probably won't even attack."

"Still, say you'll do it. Please? It'll make me feel better."

"Oh, all right. I'll do it."

"You promise?"

"I promise. But I—"

There were footsteps. Skull loomed over them, his pale, high-cheeked face looking more cadaverous than ever in the weak moonlight. "Mad Dog—your turn for guard."

"All right," Harry said.

He got his carbine and pistol, then moved down the corral wall to where Link watched through a loophole. "I'm up," Harry said.

Link grunted and stood aside, letting Harry take his place. Link remained there, staring at the station house, apparently deep in thought.

After a second Harry said, "You know, Kiah just asked me to visit his girl if something happens to him."

"Hooray for you," Link muttered.

"I never thought about how something like that might affect my family. I guess I've been too busy worrying about myself." Harry paused. "Do you . . . do you ever worry about what will happen to your family if you don't come back?"

"What family?" Link said.

"You know—your girl, Lou."

"Why the hell should I worry about Lou? If I don't come back, she'll still be alive. That'll put her one up on me."

"What about your daughter? What's going to—"

"Who said she was my daughter?"

"Come on, everybody knows that—"

"Everybody don't know shit. And you should mind your own business."

"Suit yourself," Harry said. He turned to the loophole. Link leaned back against the picket logs, deep in thought once more.

* * *

Tom Conroy entered the station house with Skull, finishing their rounds of the station. Hicks had guard on the north side, but he had shifted his post to the corral gate so that the house lights wouldn't show through the open window and attract snipers.

Inside the house, Kimball lay under the long table, trying to sleep. Nilsson had gone back to his smithy—now that the booze was destroyed, he had no need to be around other people. For the first time since Tom had arrived at Buffalo Creek, there was no card game. Bisonette sat by himself at one of the side tables, smoking his pipe and playing solitaire.

Annie Bell sat beside Barnacle Bill Sturdivant, her eyes heavy with fatigue. Tom said, "Why don't you get some sleep, Miss Bell? I'm sorry I can't offer you any privacy, but——"

"She can use my house," Bisonette said from the card table. Annie looked over at him, and he said, "Go on, it's all right. A lady deserves to be alone."

"Thank you," Annie said wearily. She rose and went next door.

To Tom, Skull said, "You should get some sleep yourself, sir. I'll call you if anything happens."

Tom shook his head. "No, I better not . . ."

"It's all right, sir. Trust me. Things should be quiet for a while, and you'll need to be rested when the fun starts."

"Very well," Tom said reluctantly.

As Skull left the station house, Tom sank down against the sod wall. He took off his forage cap. Using the satchel full of money as a pillow, he laid his head on it and closed his eyes. At least the damn bag was good for something . . .

Along the west wall, between the garden and the smithy, Acting Corporal Frazer huddled with his friend Thomas Moonlight.

"Back in New York, we call this a mug's game,"

CONROY'S FIRST COMMAND   103

Moonlight complained. "Sittin' here like this, waitin' to be killed. And for what? Sixteen dollars a month and bad food. There's fifty thousand dollars not a hundred yards from here, and we ain't allowed to touch it. Boy Wonder shouldn't give that money to no whore. It ain't right. We're the ones doing the fighting."

"I agree," Frazer said. "Lieutenant Conroy hasn't the slightest concept of how to exercise command. That money should be ours by the laws of war. The woman should be ours, as well."

"Now you're talking. I wish to hell it was you running this company."

"So do I. Things would be different then."

"Yeah, but you ain't runnin' it. I'm tellin' you, Frazer, the army ain't for me. Outside of you, the only one I liked here was Frankie Walsh, and he's dead. I'm gettin' out."

"Deserting?"

"Damn right."

"I'm curious," Frazer said. "You served in the war; you knew what the army was like. Why'd you join up again?"

"I got in trouble with the law. Armed robbery. I figured I'd let the army transport me out West, then I'd take the bounce."

"Sounds like you have it all figured out."

Moonlight snorted. "I had me enough practice. I was a bounty jumper in the war."

Bounty jumpers were men who signed up for the enlistment bonus, then deserted after receiving it and joined another regiment under a different name. "How many times did you join up?" Frazer asked him.

"Seven, I think. I was havin' so much fun, I lost count."

Frazer nodded thoughtfully. "That's interesting. Now, me, I was allowed to resign my commission. There was a problem with missing regimental funds—though I was never convicted of anything, and there's nothing on my

record to show I was suspected. That's the deal I made
with them."

"So how come *you're* back?"

"Alas, those regimental funds finally ran out. I'm a
lawyer by training, but I liked military life, so I rejoined.
I figured that, with my education and experience, I'd be
able to win a commission again." He paused. "But, you
know, I've been thinking. That fifty thousand dollars—
it's a shame to see it wasted on a whore, and there's no
reason you and I should share it with the rest of the
company. It would go a lot further split two ways, don't
you think?"

"What are you driving at?"

"Why don't you and I take that money and light out?
The hell with my commission. I'll never get one
anyway—an army that makes officers out of fools like
Conroy doesn't need me. You said you were going to de-
sert. Why not do it now, as a rich man?"

Moonlight didn't know. "That would be damn dangerous, the way things are."

"No more dangerous than staying here. Maybe less so.
If those Indians attack tomorrow, everybody here is
likely to be killed."

"What do we do about Boy Wonder? He's got the
money."

Frazer smiled. "Lieutenant Conroy is like any other
military asset—he's expendable."

Moonlight rubbed his jaw. "When do you want to do
it?"

"Tonight—it has to be. When they're all asleep. Even
if they live through this, it'll be a long time before they
can get up a pursuit. By then we'll be far away. What do
you say?"

Moonlight thought for a minute, then he grinned and
held out a hand. "I knew you should've been runnin'
this outfit, Frazer. You're a fella with vision."

There was a noise from beyond the corral wall.

"What's that?" Moonlight said as both men grabbed their carbines.

They heard it again, a muffled clip-clop. "It's a horse," Frazer said.

"Injuns?"

"Don't know. Sounds like it's shod." Frazer turned and in a loud whisper called, "Sergeant Anders!"

Others had heard the noise by now. "Turn to!" Skull ordered. Sleeping men woke. Everyone took their positions. Lieutenant Conroy came from the station house, still carrying the satchel full of money.

The horse walked parallel to the corral wall, turning the northwest corner of the station. Men peered through the loopholes. "See him?" Pennock asked.

"Yeah, yeah," Hunter said, "there he is. It's just one."

"What's he want?"

"I don't know, asshole. Why don't you ask him?"

Skull raised his voice. "Who goes there?"

There was no answer. The horse stopped in front of the corral gate. "Shall I open the gate, sir?" Skull asked Tom.

"It might be a trick," Frazer warned.

Tom said, "Sergeant, I want your four best men at the gate, ready to fire. Everybody else is to be on alert at their posts."

"Yes, sir."

Skull gave the orders. Through the loopholes men still couldn't get a clear view of the rider. "Looks like he's hurt," Hicks said. "I think I see an arrow."

When all was ready, Tom said, "Open the gate."

Hicks unbarred the gate and opened it. Link, Hunter, the Professor, and Harry stared down the barrels of their cocked Spencers, ready for anything.

The horse walked through the gate into the corral. It was one of Bisonette's horses, and it was coming home. Zurawik was tied on its back. The young Pole was naked and stuck full of arrows. His head lolled obscenely to one side, where it had nearly been sliced off.

"I guess we can forget about the relief column," Hunter said.

22

While Hicks shut the corral gate, many of the men left their stations and gathered around Zurawik's body, as though drawn to the ghastly sight involuntarily. "We're all going to be killed!" cried the telegrapher Pemberton.

Tom grabbed the young man by the shoulders. "Get a hold of yourself, Pemberton. We've got to keep our heads. That's why the Indians did this—to scare us."

"Well, it's worked pretty good on me, I can tell you," Pemberton said.

Bisonette and Annie Bell came outside. Annie was rubbing sleep from her eyes. "Don't let her see this," Tom warned Skull.

The ex-Legionnaire took Annie's arm. "Come away now, *chérie*. There is nothing for you here."

Through the crowd, Annie caught a glimpse of Zurawik's pale body. "My God, is that the man who—"

"Yes, that is the one. Go back now. You don't want to see him."

While Hunter held the horse's reins, Link and the Professor cut Zurawik's mutilated body from the saddle. The journalist Stanley Kimball came out. When he saw what the Indians had done to Zurawik, he grabbed his mouth and bent over, retching.

"Don't get much of this back East, do you?" Link asked him as he and the Professor lowered the body to the ground.

Tom raised his voice, "You men, get back to your posts. Full alert. Hayward, Woodruff—put Zurawik in the garden. We'll bury him when we get a chance."

The men hurried back to their positions, expecting an attack. Young Pemberton remained behind. He looked at Tom, wide-eyed. "Do we have any chance at all, Lieutenant?"

"We'll have a better chance if you get to your post," Tom told him. "Go on, now."

The men waited at the corral loopholes and station windows, but nothing happened. The night was quiet. Even the Indian snipers had stopped firing. At last Tom let the men stand down, save for the guards. Zurawik was buried, and silence descended on the station.

23

Midnight.

Annie Bell lay sleeping in Bisonette's house, behind the oilcloth partition, in his bed.

Suddenly, a rough hand was clamped across her mouth. Her eyes opened. She mumbled a scream, trying to get up. Then her arms were pinioned to the bed. A heavy weight fell on top of her. Foul-smelling, bearded lips pressed upon hers.

It was Bisonette. Annie tried to get away, but she was held fast to the straw-filled bed. Bisonette's lips ground into her mouth, tongue jutting, hands roaming her body. He made grunting, animal sounds, fumbling at her clothes.

Annie thrashed wildly. She threw Bisonette off and

tried to run, but he grabbed her wrist. The two of them stumbled around the small room, bouncing off the wall, tearing down the partition. Bisonette caught Annie's other wrist and wrestled her to the floor, falling on top of her. Her resistance seemed to excite him. His teeth sawed through her lower lip. She felt blood squirt.

"No," she cried. "No."

"Told you," he grunted. "I want you, and I'm going to have you."

She tried to kick him and slide from beneath him, but he wedged himself between her legs. He grabbed great handfuls of her hair and began banging her head against the earthen floor.

Annie lay dazed, stunned. Bisonette let go of her hair and ran his hands up under her dress, across her thighs, her buttocks, between her legs ...

Strong hands grabbed Bisonette by the collar and hauled him off her. Tom Conroy spun the station owner around and hit him in the face with his right hand, staggering him across the floor. Tom followed and smashed Bisonette with a left and another right as he came off the wall. Bisonette crumpled to the floor. He tried to get up, and Tom kicked him in the pit of the stomach, lifting him into the air and onto his back, where he lay moaning.

Tom bent over, breathing hard. "You son of a bitch." He turned toward Annie. As he did, Bisonette rolled over and drew his pistol.

"Lieutenant!" Annie cried.

Tom turned back, kicking Bisonette's gun hand aside just as he fired. Tom's kick sent the pistol flying, and he picked it up and held it on Bisonette, who stared up at him malevolently. Tom's right hand hurt like hell; he hoped he hadn't broken it.

Skull burst through the back door, carbine ready. He looked around. "Everything all right, sir?"

"Everything's fine, Sergeant," Tom replied, puffing. "I'll handle this."

"You sure, sir?"

"I'm sure. As you were."

Skull noted Bisonette's battered condition and he raised an amused eyebrow. "Yes, sir." He went back outside.

Nearby, Annie pulled herself to her feet. Bisonette came to one elbow, wiping blood from his mouth with his free hand. "God damn you, Lieutenant. I didn't do nothing."

"You call rape 'nothing'?"

Bisonette spat blood and sat up. "You can't rape a whore. Even the courts say that ain't no crime."

Tom almost shot Bisonette right there, but his hand hurt so much he wasn't sure he could pull the trigger. "Get out," he told Bisonette.

Bisonette staggered to his feet. "I'll go. I'll go. But I'll get you for this." He tapped the mysterious deerskin pouch that hung at his belt.

"What's in that pouch, anyway?" Tom asked.

"None of your—"

Putting down the pistol, Tom grabbed the station owner by the shirt and hurled him against the wall so hard that the room shook. The air was knocked from Bisonette's lungs. He stood against the wall, helpless, while Tom tore the pouch from his belt. The pouch was surprisingly light. Tom opened it and poured its contents into his hand.

It was a pile of human ears. The ears were dried and shriveled, save for two that looked fairly fresh. Tom looked at them and his stomach curled.

Opposite him, Bisonette smiled. "From the men I killed. Little trophies."

"You're sick," Tom told him.

"Why? Indians take scalps, and we call them great warriors. This is my version of scalps. Your ears will be there one day, too."

Tom went to the window, opened it, and threw the

ears into the night. He tossed the empty pouch to
Bisonette. "You'll have to start a new collection."

"I don't mind. Just remember whose ears will be
first."

"I wouldn't count on that," Tom said. "Now, get out
of here. And keep away from Miss Bell." Tom turned
the station owner around, put a boot to his rear and pro-
pelled him through the back door.

Sergeant Anders stuck his head back in. "Want me to
put that fellow under arrest, sir?"

Tom considered, while he tried to shake the pain from
his right hand. "No," he decided, "I don't think he'll try
anything else—for now. We'll need him if there's an attack. Just keep an eye on him."

Skull touched his hat brim. "Yes, sir."

As Skull stepped away, Tom turned to Annie. "Are
you . . . are you all right?"

"I think so," she replied. Her scalp hurt; Bisonette had
nearly pulled the hair out of her head. Her lower lip was
swelling, and there was blood down her chin and the
front of her blouse. She had assorted other bumps and
bruises, and her knees were suddenly very shaky.

Tom assisted her to the room's only chair. "You'd better sit."

He couldn't light a lantern because of the Indians. By
the dim light from the distant campfires, he examined
the inch-long gash on her lip. "Let me clean that."

"No, that's all—"

"Just hold still and let me do it."

He ransacked Bisonette's trunk, found what he hoped
was a clean towel, and wet it from the water jug. Holding Annie's chin, he dabbed away the blood. There was
a trickle of blood from her nose, and he wiped that away,
too. He folded the towel and pressed it against her lip.
"Hold that there till it stops bleeding."

Annie did so. With her free hand, she attempted to
straighten her disheveled hair, wincing from the pain. "I

must thank you, Lieutenant," she mumbled through her towel-covered mouth.

"That's all right," Tom said. He flexed his throbbing right hand, touchiing the swollen knuckles gingerly. It had felt good to hit that bastard. He wished he'd done it two weeks ago. "I couldn't sleep. I heard the racket over here. Something told me what was happening."

"If you hadn't come along . . ."

"Try not to think about it. Its over now."

She attempted a smile. "No lectures about how much trouble I am?"

"No lectures," Tom said. He added, "Look, I have to . . . I have to apologize. For the way I've treated you. You did nothing to deserve it, and I'm sorry. I should have been praising you, if anything. You shouldered a rifle with the rest, and God knows you've been a big help with the wounded."

She shrugged. "I see the same thing most every Saturday night." She put down the bloodstained towel and rose unsteadily. "I need some fresh air. I can't stand to be in this room another second."

"Maybe I—maybe I should come with you," Tom offered. "In case you need help."

"All right," Annie said.

Tom picked up the satchel full of money that he had left by the door, then he and Annie went outside.

24

Tom held the satchel in his left hand; his right hand hurt too much. "Do you take that bag everywhere?" Annie asked him.

"If I didn't, it would be empty in five minutes," Tom replied.

"Couldn't you leave it with your sergeant?"

"I don't trust him any more than I do the others—a lot less than some of them, in fact."

"Have you no thoughts of taking the money for yourself?"

"I've been around money all my life. I guess it doesn't mean that much to me. Besides, I'm an officer. Stealing your money would be dishonorable."

She looked surprised. "Do you really believe in things like honor?"

"It's my job to believe in those things."

Annie half closed her eyes and breathed deeply. Her hair stuck up at all angles where Bisonette had pulled it. Her clothes were torn and there was blood down the front of her white blouse. Blood had started dripping from her gashed underlip again, and she wiped it on her sleeve.

The flurry of excitement caused by the gunshot had passed. The station had returned to the quiet depths of night. Overhead the stars sparkled among drifting clouds. In the yard there were snatches of movement from the guards and the one or two men who were not asleep. In

the stables a horse shuffled. There was no sign of
Bisonette; he must have returned to the station house.

Annie and Tom began walking. To Tom the setting
was surreal. He might have been strolling the parade
ground at Fort Pierce with a brother officer's wife or visiting sister, making polite conversation; in reality he was
circling the corral of a stage station about to be overrun
by Indians, talking to a whore. He felt sudden sympathy
for this young woman, old beyond her years. "I have to
admire the way you've held up, after what you've been
through."

"I'm used to adversity," she said.

"Still, that's a fair amount of adversity for one day—
attacked by Indians, losing your man, nearly raped."

She looked over, weary, correcting a mistake. "Johnny
wasn't my man, not in the sense you mean. He was just
a good friend."

"Oh," Tom said. "I was under the impression that you
and he were . . ."

"Lovers? We were, sometimes, when it suited us—out
of loneliness, or desperation, or whatever it is that people
in our business feel. But there was no commitment, no
sense that we couldn't be with others when it suited us.
Our relationship was strictly professional." She smiled
wanly. "I guess that sounds shocking?"

"I'm not as easily shocked as I used to be," Tom said.

They passed the stables and turned along the south
wall. "It's so peaceful," Annie sighed, "like the danger
was far away. You could almost forget what's happened
today. You could almost forget what's going to happen
tomorrow."

"Maybe nothing will happen," Tom suggested.
"Maybe the Indians will just ride away."

"I don't think either of us believes that."

They kept walking, the shuffle of their feet a rhythmic
accompaniment to the night's stillness. "How long had
you known Mr. Lowe?" Tom asked.

"Five years. We started working together in Springfield, during the war. We'd rent space in a saloon or gambling hall. I'd shill for his business, he'd protect me in mine. We made a good team. We left right after Bill Hickok shot Dave Tutt and the authorities started clamping down. We went to Kansas City, and when the authorities started clamping down *there*, we struck out for Denver."

"And before you met Lowe?" Tom asked, interested in knowing now, not just making conversation.

"I did a lot of things in a lot of places, most of which I'd rather forget." She brightened a bit. "I was born in Scotland, you know."

"Really?"

"I don't remember it, of course. We came to the States when I was little. My parents died in some kind of plague not long after that, and I was raised by neighbors. When I was thirteen, I had some 'trouble' with my stepfather, and I ran away. I got a job in a big New York house, working as a lady's maid. Then I had some 'trouble' with the master. Of course the lady found out about it, and of course she blamed me, so I was dismissed. By then there wasn't much other work open to me. Besides, I figured that if I was going to be having all this 'trouble' with men, I might as well get paid for it. I tried to make a go on the streets, but that's impossible, so I worked for a lousy succession of pimps and madames. But all the while I was doing it, I swore that some day, somehow, I would gain control over my life. Then I met Johnny, and everything changed. Now I'm in a position to control my life, but he isn't here to see it. I'll miss him."

They finished their circuit of the corral. "Do you mind if we sit?" Annie asked. "My legs feel kind of weak."

"Certainly," Tom said. "Shall we go inside?"

"I'd rather stay out here. It's a nice evening. And if we go inside, I might see Bisonette again, and I don't think I could handle that right now."

Tom led her to the sheltered space between the stables

and the smithy. She sat against the corral wall, legs drawn up girlishly beneath her. Tom put down the satchel and sat with his back to the stables' adobe wall. "Enough about me," Annie said. "What about you? You're West Point, I assume?"

Tom shook his head. "Yale."

"Yale? But why are you—"

"In the army? Sometimes I wonder. I joined to prove myself, I guess. To show that there was something I could do on my own. It's not always easy being born with a silver spoon in your mouth."

"I'd like to have tried it."

"I won't deny it has its advantages, but there's drawbacks, too. You never know whether what you've accomplished has been through your own efforts or because of your family. All my life I've been who my family wanted me to be. I never really knew who I was or what I wanted to do. I never had a chance to find out. Joining the army was an attempt to get away from all that."

"Your family was against it?"

Tom laughed. "My family thinks I should be committed. 'Why do you want to be a soldier?' they said. 'The war is over. Consider the social position this puts us in. Why can't you just be a lawyer, join the firm, and be done with it?' Finally my father saw that I wouldn't change my mind, and he tried to get me into one of the fashionable regiments back East. But I wanted the cavalry, where the action was. So I used his connections and wangled myself an appointment to the Fifth."

He paused, looking away. "'I used his connections'—that's a pathetic admission, isn't it? I couldn't even do this on my own."

"Yes, but you're here now," Annie said. "That's what matters."

"And now I wonder if I did the right thing. I wonder what business I have telling these boys to get killed."

"I think you're doing an excellent job," she said.

"Really?"

"Really. You'll see—someday you'll look back on your performance here with pride."

"Look back from where—the grave?" Hastily, Tom added, "Sorry. I didn't mean to upset you."

"I'm not upset. I know what can happen to us."

"You don't seem worried."

"I'm an optimist. You have to be in my line of work."

Annie's lip was bleeding again. She wiped it on the back of her hand, blood smearing her chin. "You should have that sewn," Tom told her.

She shrugged. "Be a nice scar either way." Then she said, "How's your hand doing?" She took his swollen right hand in both of her own. The soft pressure of her hands felt strange on his. Gently she touched his knuckles, and he winced. "And *you* should have this iced," she told him, "or at least put in cold water."

Tom said nothing. She did not let go of his hand, and he did not want her to. She said, "Why don't I wet a cloth and wrap this for you? It might help some."

"I'd prefer it if you just stayed here," Tom replied, heart racing.

She cocked her head to one side. "Would you?"

"Yes. I'd rather talk to you than have you worry about my hand."

"I'd like that, too," she said. She edged closer to him, still holding his hand.

"Sorry to interrupt," a voice said.

They turned. The voice belonged to Acting Corporal Frazer. He and Private Moonlight stood in the shadows between the stables and the smithy, with their carbines trained on Tom and Annie.

25

Tom rose. "What the—"

Frazer cut him off. "We want the money, Lieutenant. Give it to us and we won't shoot you."

"Put down those weapons and return to your posts. That's an order."

"We don't take orders no more," Moonlight said, grinning. "We done discharged ourselves."

"And if I won't give you the money?" Tom asked.

Frazer was grim. "We're taking it, one way or the other."

"You'll never make it to the horses and out the gate."

"We're not going out the gate. We're going over the wall."

"That's suicide."

"No more suicide than staying here," Frazer said. "We'll make our way upriver, then hide out till we can join an emigrant train. If we give 'em money, they won't ask questions." He raised his carbine. "Last chance, Lieutenant. We don't have any more time."

Tom stepped in front of the leather satchel, his chest stiffening with pride and anger. "I guess you'll have to—"

Annie grabbed his arm. "No. It's only money, let them have it. It's not worth your life."

Tom said nothing; he kept looking at Frazer and Moonlight.

"Please," Annie begged, "do it for me. It's my money, after all. I should have some say in what happens to it."

"Lady's got some sense," Moonlight told Tom. "Best listen to her."

At last Tom let out his breath. "Very well." He felt humiliated, defeated, inadequate.

"Good," Frazer said. "Take out your revolver, put it on the ground, and kick it this way."

Tom did.

"Now the bag."

With his foot, Tom pushed the satchel toward Frazer.

Frazer picked up the satchel, smiling. "Thanks, Lieutenant. Now, we'll be on our way, and you two lovebirds can—"

"Nice play, boys," said a voice from the rear. "But it won't work."

Frazer and Moonlight turned. "Hayward," breathed Moonlight.

Link stood with his carbine in his hands. On his lips was the faintest suggestion of a smile. Frazer kept his voice down, so no one else in the station would hear. "There's no need for trouble, Hayward. There's plenty of money. Come with us, and we'll split it three ways."

"No, thanks," Link replied.

"You can't fight us, Hayward," Moonlight warned. "It's two against one."

"Not now it isn't," said another voice, and Harry Winston stepped out of the shadows behind Link.

Link looked surprised to see Harry, but he recovered quickly. "What's it going to be, General?" he asked Frazer.

Abruptly, Frazer slipped behind Annie, grabbing her around the shoulders with one arm, holding his carbine barrel to her head with the other. "You'll have to shoot her to get me," he said.

"That won't bother me," Link replied.

Frazer saw that he meant it. He hesitated, unsure what to do. At that moment Tom threw himself at Frazer's gun arm, yanking it down. Annie twisted away from

Frazer and dropped to the ground. Moonlight, Link, and Harry all fired together. Moonlight cried out and fell.

Frazer stumbled around with Tom, then clubbed Tom's jaw with the carbine butt, knocking him down. Frazer turned to fire and was caught by shots from Link and Harry. He staggered back against the corral wall. Link fired again, and Frazer pitched onto his face.

Annie rose and knelt beside Tom. "Are you all right?"

Tom blinked his eyes, trying to focus them. "I think so."

Harry and Link checked the fallen men. "This one's dead," Harry said of Moonlight.

"So's this one," Link said, turning Frazer over.

Link hurried and picked up the satchel as Skull, Hunter, and some other men came running up. Skull looked around. "All right, sir?" he asked Tom.

Tom nodded, standing with Annie's help.

Skull went on. "What happened?"

Harry answered for Tom. "The General and Moonlight here tried to take the lady's money."

"Bad apples," Skull said. "I knew it all along. We're well rid of them."

"Maybe," Tom said, wiggling his sore jaw, "but it gives us two less men to hold the perimeter when the Indians come." To Harry he said, "Winston, you have my thanks. Hayward, too—where is he?"

Link came up from behind the others and handed the satchel to Tom. "It was nothing, sir. Just doing our job."

A crowd gathered between the stables and the smithy, gesturing and talking, some rubbing sleep from their eyes. Bisonette, Hicks, and the blacksmith Nilsson were there, with about half the soldiers. When they saw the two bodies, the noise level rose. Tom said, "Sergeant, see that these two are buried. Get the rest of the men back to their posts. I want a full alert starting at an hour before dawn. Make Campbell acting corporal of Second Squad."

"Yes, sir," Skull replied. He turned, "All right, men,

back to your posts. The show is over. *Acting Corporal* Hunter, O'Meara, Peel—take those bodies. Pemberton, you help them—no reason civilians can't do a little work around here. Peel, when you're done, you'll take Frazer's and Moonlight's post by the garden."

"The garden—right, Sarge," Useless Peel said.

"Make sure that weapon's clean."

"It is, Sarge."

"Corporal Hartz—see to the dead men's weapons. Distribute their ammunition among the rest of the platoon."

"Got it, Sarge."

The detailed men picked up the bodies, and the small crowd melted away, leaving Tom and Annie alone.

Annie was shaking. She still felt the cold steel of the carbine barrel pressed against her temple. Tom put his arms around her, comforting her. She buried her head against his chest, absorbing strength from him.

After a moment she looked up. The two of them stared into each others' eyes, hesitant, searching for something. Then they kissed.

26

Link and Harry crossed the corral yard, returning to their posts on the east wall. "What made you go over there?" Harry asked Link.

Link shrugged. "I never did trust them two. I went to stop them from taking the money." He paused. "What were you doing there?"

"I went to stop *you* from taking the money."

Link halted and turned. "What are you saying, you rookie bag of shit?"

"You know damn well what I'm saying," Harry told him. "I think you were planning to steal that money for yourself, but Frazer and Midnight beat you to it. And don't give me that 'rookie' crap. I've proved myself. If it wasn't for me, you'd be dead at the bottom of Cheyenne Bluff right now—or don't you remember how I saved your ass? I'm still trying to figure out how we got separated when we went down the bluff for water."

"Just good luck, I guess," Link said with a smirk, and he walked away.

Nearby, the burial detail was digging two new graves. "This garden's growing more bodies than it is vegetables," Hunter said as he eyed the lengthening row of dirt mounds.

Useless Peel wrapped blankets around the bodies of Frazer and Moonlight. "It's fixin' to grow more, I'm afeared."

"I reckon we'll all be in here before it's over," said the telegrapher Pemberton.

"Almost makes you want to die now, and save yourself the digging," Hunter said.

O'Meara leaned on his shovel. "That presents an interesting conundrum, does it not? If our young friend's prophecy comes true, who d'ye reckon will bury the last man?"

"I don't know, but I guarantee you it won't be the Injuns," Hunter said. "By the way, what the hell is a 'conundrum'?"

It was a soft, lingering kiss, and when it ended there was another. At last their lips drew apart, and they faced each other with amazement.

"I've never been kissed like that before," Annie whispered. "It's always been business with me. You make me feel different—like a woman."

"I feel like a kid at Christmas," Tom admitted, "all giddy and excited. I wish we could make this moment last forever."

"Nothing lasts forever," she said wistfully.

Tom smoothed the dark, lustrous hair that Bisonette had so brutally pulled, then he ran his fingertips across her high cheekbones. "I've known you less than a day, but I feel like I've known you all my life. I can talk to you in a way I never talked with other people. It's like I can tell you anything, things I never told anyone before. But we have so little time. It doesn't seem—"

Annie pushed back from him.

"What's wrong?" Tom asked

She looked away. "Just when I've finally gotten control of my life, I'm losing it again—to another person, to an emotion. I don't know if I'm ready for that, I don't know if I'll ever be ready. I feel like I'm about to unlock something I've kept hidden inside me all these years, and I'm not sure I'm ready for that, either. I once promised that I'd never make a commitment to anyone but myself, and here I go breaking that promise. It's all so sudden, so unexpected."

"So unwanted?"

"I didn't say that. It's just that we're so different."

"I know. Me, the spoiled rich boy; you, the—well, you know. It's crazy."

"You're wondering if this is real, or if it's a reaction to what's going on around us."

"It seems real to me," he said.

"It seems real to me, too."

He moved closer to her. "So what do we do about it?"

She smiled. "For starters, you can stop calling me 'Miss Bell' and start calling me Annie."

"Only if you'll stop calling me 'Lieutenant' and start calling me Tom."

"It's a deal—Tom."

They laughed at the pure childishness of it all. She took his hands. "Ow!" he yelped.

Annie put a hand across her mouth, biting her lip and laughing like a schoolgirl. "Oh, my God, I'm sorry. I forgot you're hurt. Are you all right?"

Tom took her arm and pulled her close, feeling the curves of her body press against him. "I will be in a minute," he told her.

Their lips met again. Then, from the east wall of the station, came a cry. Tom twisted around in time to see a point of light flare, die, then flare briefly again. More points of light arced into the night sky around them.

"Fire arrows!" someone shouted. "They're shooting fire arrows!"

27

"They're not waiting for dawn," Tom swore. He heard his men yelling at one another to take their positions. A rifle shot sounded from the nearby smithy.

Tom took Annie's shoulders. "Go to the station house."

She protested. "Can't I stay with—"

"No," he told her. He led her to the edge of the stables and handed her the satchel with the money. "I'll see you when I can." He kissed her, hoping it was not their last kiss, then he said, "Now, get going."

As Annie hurried off, Tom strode across the corral yard. "Sergeant Anders!"

The ex-Legionnaire materialized at Tom's shoulder. "Sir?"

"Are the men ready?"

"Ready as they can be, sir."

Tom peered through a loophole in the wall. The Indians were lighting the arrows from their campfires, then riding forward and shooting the arrows into the compound. Tom's men had begun shooting at the points of light bobbing up and down outside.

"Don't fire unless you have a good target," Tom ordered. "We're low on ammunition." Amazing how many times you had to repeat things. Some of these men would blaze away all their bullets in minutes if allowed to. "One man per wall is to shoot, Sergeant. The rest prepare to fight fires."

"Yes, sir," Skull said.

Arrows were flying into the compound from three sides—the fourth side was guarded by the fireproof sod houses. The arrows hissed through the air, leaving trails of sparks. Some fell harmlessly into the dirt of the corral. Others thunked into the palisaded walls, where some burned out but others caught fire in the dry wood and flared up. The men stacked crates and boxes, climbed up on them, and leaned over the walls to beat at the flames with their jackets.

"Come on," Tom told Skull.

He led his sergeant to the storehouse. The door had been locked, but Tom shot off the lock with his pistol. "Very good, sir," Skull remarked. "You're getting the hang of this officer thing."

Inside, Tom struck a match, found what he was looking for, and began pulling down stacks of trade blankets. "We'll use these on the fires."

"What about water, sir?"

"There's not enough of us for a bucket brigade."

Skull clucked. "Bisonette's probably going to complain about us ruining his blankets to keep his station from burning down."

Tom took one of the gray blankets. He lit another match and motioned to Skull to look. The blanket had "U.S." stamped on its corner.

"The son of a bitch," Skull marveled. "He stole them from the army."

Tom and Skull each took an armload of the blankets and went back outside. Tom said, "When these are given out, I'll help on the south wall, you take the west."

"Right, sir."

The fire arrows kept coming. In the stables the terrified horses snorted and reared and kicked at their stalls. On the east wall Harry, Kiah, and O'Meara fought the flames, while Link fired through the loopholes at the Indians who were bringing the fire arrows forward. A stationary point of light on the ground told where he had hit one of them.

Harry leaned far over the palisaded wall, beating at a flaming arrow with his blanket, knocking it out of the wall and onto the ground. Battle madness had come over Harry again, like it had on Cheyenne Bluff, that strange mixture of terror and elation that jolted his body with a crazy energy, a frantic desire to live combined with a complete indifference to death. He seemed to be inside himself and outside himself at the same time. He saw things with the utmost clarity, and at the same time he was in a fog.

The men were able to extinguish the arrows higher up on the walls, but they couldn't reach the ones lower down. Flames spread along the bases of the walls. The men beat at them as they rose higher, and beat at them from inside as they licked through the spaces between the logs. It was hot work. The men were coughing and choking from the smoke and flames. An entire section of the south wall was on fire now.

Then an arrow hit the haystack that was kept outside the station, opposite the south wall. The hay went up in flames, illuminating the station in its flickering red glare, casting long shadows across the yard. The breeze blew sparks from the burning haystack down onto the compound. Along the south wall the sparks caught and grew into flames. More sparks popped and cracked from the dry wood. Dutch Hartz stopped firing. He, Tom, the Professor, and Cuddy had all they could do to hold the flames in check. As fast as they put out one fire, another—or even two—took its place.

From the darkness outside the station other Indians began shooting rifles and arrows at the compound. Bullets whizzed around the men's heads or buried themselves in the palisade walls. Arrows dropped seemingly from out of nowhere. Fire had taken hold on the east wall now. A dense pall of smoke from the hay rack drifted over the station, making it hard for the defenders to see their hands in front of their faces. On the west wall, Hunter and Pennock climbed onto the stable roof to get above the smoke. In the glare from the burning hay loft, they saw figures darting across the open ground toward the station.

"They're attacking!" Hunter cried.

The Indians were advancing on foot, looking for openings in the burning walls, firing at the firefighters and at gun flashes from the loopholes. "That bastard Storm has them fighting like white men," Hunter shouted to Pennock as he fired down at the attackers.

Men left the losing battle with the flames to open fire with their carbines—some because they were scared of the Indians, some because they were too exhausted to swing blankets anymore. Link barely missed being shot as an Indian stuck a pistol through his loophole and fired just at the moment he turned away to reload. By the time Link got back to the loophole, the Indian was gone.

"Maintain the perimeter!" Tom cried. He wanted to wait as long as he could before withdrawing. He wanted to make the Indians battle for every inch of the station. If the price they paid was high enough, maybe they would get tired and go away. It was still a long time till dawn—this was not the Indians' usual way of fighting.

Suddenly, the Indians across from the north wall of the station, who had been quiet thus far, opened up with a well-aimed barrage of rifle and pistol fire, driving the defenders in both the station house and Bisonette's house away from their windows and loopholes. As the defenders' return fire faded, two Indians ran forward. They were Sliding Down Hill and his friend Two Bears. Man Alone, the war party's leader, had been impressed with Sliding Down Hill, and he had given the young Cheyenne and his friend the most important role in the attack.

Sliding Down Hill and Two Bears stopped by the corral gate. Each carried a looped rope in his hand and a knife in his teeth. The two young warriors tossed the ropes up until the loops caught around the ends of the logs, then they began climbing, racing each other to the top. Laughing, Two Bears reached the top first and threw himself over the other side.

Hicks, the station attendant, was at his position by the gate. Keeping his head down because of the intense gunfire from across the road, he was watching the soldiers battle the flames around the corral yard when he sensed a presence above him. He rose and looked up just as Two Bears jumped down. Hicks fired his repeater. The bullet entered the falling Indian's stomach, blasted up through his body and came out the back of his neck. He fell on Hicks, knocking him down. The white man recovered and pumped another shot into Two Bears. As he did, Sliding Down Hill drew his knife and leaped from the gate top. He landed on the balls of his feet, plunging his knife into Hicks's throat. The white man gargled, staggered around, and fell thrashing.

Sliding Down Hill moved to open the gate. Only one white soldier had seen what had occurred. Useless Peel left his post by the garden and came running, his carbine leveled. Sliding Down Hill turned. The soldier pulled the trigger; the hammer snapped but the weapon did not fire. The soldier kept coming. Sliding Down Hill drew his pistol from his belt. The soldier pointed the carbine at the charm on Sliding Down Hill's chest and pulled the trigger again. Again the hammer snapped, but the weapon did not fire. Sliding Down Hill raised his pistol and fired at almost point-blank range. A crimson flower blossomed on Peel's pale forehead and he flopped over backward, dropping his dirty rifle.

Sliding Down Hill turned again, lifting the heavy bar from the gate. He set the bar down and swung the gate open. There was a triumphant yell from across the road, and dozens of mounted Indians galloped out of the darkness and into the station yard.

28

Shots from the houses on each side of the gate dropped a few of the mounted Indians, but not enough to stop the attack.

Tom was fighting fires with the men on the south wall when he heard horses behind him. He turned and saw the Indians pouring through the corral gate. They were yelling and shooting, and the only reason his whole command wasn't killed on the spot was because of the night-time darkness and the dense smoke. Tom threw away his blanket. "Corporal Hartz. Take your squad and withdraw to the station house. Keep to the corral walls and stay together as best you can. I'm going to tell the others."

"Yes, sir," Dutch said. As Tom moved off, Dutch said, "Professor, Cuddy—you heard him. Time to go."

The three men grabbed their carbines and started off, trying to stay hidden in the smoke and dust and confusion. As they reached the east wall, Dutch yelled, "Link, where are you?"

"Over here."

Dutch waved his men forward. His eyes were burning, his lungs full of hot smoke. "Mad Dog, Kiah, O'Meara—back to the station house. Hurry."

Tom reached the stables. Somebody shot at him as he ran by, but he paid no attention. "Campbell, Pennock?" he called.

"Up here, sir," Hunter shouted from the stable roof.

"Retreat to the station house. Get Peel on your way."

"Yes, sir."

Skull appeared at Tom's elbow. He had lost his hat, and in his cadaverous face his eyes burned with the flame of battle. "I'll tell that blacksmith," he said.

Skull stuck his head into the smithy, where the blacksmith was shooting through his shuttered window. "Nilsson, we're pulling back to the station house."

Nilsson fired again.

"Nilsson—did you hear me?"

"I heard you," the blacksmith replied without looking. "I'll come in a second." He reloaded and fired again.

Skull went back outside. As he did, a bullet shattered his right collarbone and he cried out.

Tom came up. "Are you hit bad?"

Skull bent over, holding his shoulder. "I'll be all right," he replied through gritted teeth. "Damn, I'm getting tired of this."

Tom holstered his pistol and retrieved the wounded man's carbine. "Put your good arm around my shoulder," he told Skull.

The two men made their way along the wall to Bisonette's house. Tom's lungs grabbed for oxygen in the smoke, his legs ached from Anders's weight. Figures swirled around them in the smoke. Tom heard bullets hum past him, and he thanked God for the bad visibility. Bisonette's house loomed out of the murk. The back door was open, and Bisonette was firing through it. The bullet brushed Tom's hair. Tom's eyes met Bisonette's, and the hatred he found there made Tom wonder if the bullet had been meant for him. Then another man appeared at the opening—Pemberton—and the look on Bisonette's face changed. Tom picked up his pace and fell through the door with his burden.

Atop the stables, Hunter hit Pennock on the shoulder. "Let's go."

Hunter hooked his carbine to its sling. Crouching, he ran to the edge of the building and jumped off. More cautious, Pennock caught hold of one of the roof supports, swung out, and dropped to the corral yard, swearing.

"God damn splinter in my hand." He grimaced, shaking his right hand.

The two men unhooked their carbines from their slings and ran for the station house. As they passed the smithy they heard a rifle shot from inside, but they did not stop to investigate. Behind them there were Indians on foot, and they wanted to reach safety before the Indians caught up to them. They looked for Peel, but he wasn't at his post, and they weren't going to stand around waiting for him.

In the smithy, Lars-Erik Nilsson fired his single-shot Sharps rifle. He reloaded and fired again, unhurried. There was a pile of paper cartridges on the workbench beside him, along with enough canned food and water jugs to last a week. He had no need, or desire, to leave.

As always, Nilsson wanted to be alone with his memories—memories of Zeldah, his wife, whom he had beaten to death in a drunken rage. He had believed her to be having an affair with one of their neighbors back in Kittery, Maine. When he learned that his jealousy was unfounded, his grief had been uncontrollable and he had fled west, to escape both her memory and the law.

He had ended up at Buffalo Creek Station, drowning his sorrow in whiskey and living in fear that people would find out who he was, what he had done. He still loved Zeldah, he always would. Now he preferred to make his stand here in the smithy, by himself, the way he had done everything since she died. Smoke—he thought it was smoke—made tears run down his cheeks and into his black beard. The heavy rifle butt smacked into his shoulder with each shot. The smell of powder and burning wood filled his nostrils.

An Indian entered the smithy behind Nilsson and fired a Lancaster rifle into his back. The .52 slug tore through Nilsson's kidney, making him cry out with agony and sag at the knees. Nilsson turned and saw a big Cheyenne with a war bonnet and a red shield. As the Cheyenne reloaded, another Indian—a Sioux—pushed past him with a war axe, to count coup.

Nilsson picked up his heavy hammer from his workbench. He swung it backhanded and caught the Sioux alongside the head, crushing his skull and face bones. As the Sioux fell, shrieking, Nilsson eyed the Cheyenne with the red shield. Holding the hammer, he beckoned the Cheyenne forward with his other hand. The Cheyenne raised his rifle and shot Nilsson just under the breastbone. The blacksmith's eyes opened wide, and he fell against the workbench, then to the floor.

Other warriors moved through the doorway to count coup and take the blacksmith's scalp, but Man Alone turned away. He no longer believed in counting coup or in taking scalps. He believed only in killing and death. He had fixed the white soldiers' 5/K device to the front of his war bonnet. In his fight against the white men, he was becoming like them. He sometimes wondered if victory was worth such a price.

Dutch Hartz's squad ran toward the station house, moving through smoke turned red from the fires. Around them were hideous yells, the crashing of timbers as the walls started to collapse, the screaming of horses in the stables. The Indians seemed to have little idea where the whites were. Most refused to dismount, and they fired their guns and arrows randomly around the yard.

Kiah Sanders was hit just above the ankle. He yelped and limped along, trying to keep up with the others.

"All right?" Harry asked him.

"Yeah," Kiah said.

Somehow Patrick Cuddy got turned around in the smoke. He was hurrying along when he lost contact with the others and suddenly found himself in the stables. He came face-to-face with an Indian. He shot wildly at the Indian with his carbine, turned around and ran back out into the smoke.

Still disoriented, he blundered into the middle of the yard. He was knocked down by a horse going past. He scrambled up, crying with fear. He started running again, and bumped into another horse. Its Indian rider hit him with something. Cuddy staggered but didn't fall. There was a whoop, and more Indians gathered around him, their painted faces making them look like demons from hell in the reddish smoke. One of them fired a rifle. The bullet hit Cuddy in the ribs and he yelled. He tried to keep standing but couldn't. He dropped to his knees. More rifles and arrows were fired at him until at last his lifeless body fell forward.

Trying to keep his men together, Dutch Hartz saw that Cuddy was missing. He went back for him, shouting in the smoke. "Cuddy! Cuddy!" He looked at the ground, figuring the New Yorker must have been hit. "Cuddy! Where are you?"

There was no sign of him. Dutch went back almost to where they had started before he gave up. The others were far ahead of him now. Dutch sprinted after them. He tripped and fell. He tried to get up and found he couldn't. There was a burning pain in his lower left side. He must have been shot.

He raised himself to his hands and knees. He felt sick. He forgot about the battle and his squad and getting to the station house. Alternate waves of chill and heat swept over him. He was nauseous and dizzy. His stomach heaved and he vomited blood.

"Holy Mary, mother of God . . ."

He tried to keep his eyes focused. With great effort he inched forward. He never saw the Indian who came up and knocked out his brains with a rifle butt.

Link and O'Meara ran side by side. They had stopped to fire at the Indians riding by in the smoke and had fallen behind Harry and Kiah. O'Meara had lost his cap; he was bleeding from a wound across his temple. An arrow bounced off the metal buckle of Link's carbine sling, its force punching him back a step.

The entire east wall of the corral was in flames now. The fire had spread to the kitchen and storehouse. As Link and O'Meara went by, the flames reached the powder kegs in the storehouse and they blew up. The explosion hurled Link and O'Meara through the air, singeing their hair and clothing. Indian horses screamed and reared, throwing their riders. Terrified, most of the Indians turned and rode out of the station yard. There was a massive hole in the wall where the storehouse had been.

Link and O'Meara lay flat, ears ringing, eyes temporarily blinded from the blast. Link picked himself up. "Come on," he told O'Meara, shaking the Irishman's jacket collar. He pulled O'Meara to his feet, pushing him along, though he had no idea if they were going in the right direction anymore. Then hands reached out and pulled the two men into the station house. Link stumbled into the smoke-filled room, unable to see much in the darkness, hearing the heavy breathing of others all around, smelling sweat and fear above the acrid powder stench. He realized it was Mad Dog Winston who had pulled him in; the Professor had hold of O'Meara.

"Where's the rest of them?" Mad Dog asked him.

Link shook his head dumbly.

Link's eyes cleared. Mad Dog and the Professor were at the back door. Annie Bell and Kiah, who was hurt, held the front windows. Kimball cringed in a corner. The others must be dead or in Bisonette's house, Link thought. He picked up his carbine, preparing for the Indians' final assault.

The assault didn't come. The Indians had been scared by the powder explosion, and nothing that Man Alone could do could lessen their fear. They were retreating. From the yard came the neighing of horses and hoofbeats as the Indians released the animals from the stables and ran them out the corral gates. The hoofbeats faded into the distance, and silence descended on the station.

29

The sudden silence was in some ways more terrifying than the action had been. Link stood. "Look alive," he told the men in the station house, "this ain't over. Run a patch through them carbines. Then one at a time get yourselves a drink and fill your canteens." He began poking behind the bar of the smoke-filled building, turning things over. "God damn, there must be a bottle left around this dump somewhere."

Tom Conroy squinted out the front window of Bisonette's house. His eyes burned as they tried to penetrate the smoke and darkness. If the Indians were still out there, he couldn't see them. He had left his watch in the now-destroyed camp, and because of the smoke he could not see the Dipper; he had no idea how long it was until dawn. He worried about Annie and if she was all right, even though, as a soldier, that was the last thing that should be on his mind right now. Nearby, Pennock and Hunter covered the windows. The telegrapher Pemberton was at the front door and Bisonette was at the back. Pemberton had a slight wound in his neck and another across the back of his hand. Sergeant Anders lay in the station owner's bed, bleeding all over it.

"Are they gone, sir?" Pennock asked.

"I wouldn't count on it," Tom told him. "How many bullets do you men have left?"

"Two, sir," Pennock replied.

"I got five, sir," Hunter said.

Two shells out of a hundred. Not bad really, Tom thought, considering how long they'd been in action and the firing rate of the Spencers. He reloaded his Smith & Wesson .45 pistol. "How are you doing, Sergeant?" he asked Skull.

"Fine, sir," Skull said from Bisonette's bed. "I'm just tired of being wounded everytime there's a fight. I had the same problem when I was in the Legion."

Tom moved to the back door. Bisonette let him by. The two men exchanged looks, and Tom felt anger rise within him. He couldn't look at Bisonette without remembering the station owner's boast that "you can't rape a whore," and wanting to kick his teeth out because of it. He could see that Bisonette felt the same about him.

"Keep your eyes open," he told the men. "I'm going next door."

Pistol ready, he stepped outside, half expecting Bisonette to try and shoot him in the back. After the noise and confusion of the fight, the station was eerily quiet, except for the crackle of flames in the places where the corral walls still burned. The rest of the walls were gone, smoldering embers. Aside from the two houses, all that remained of the station were the adobe stables and the smithy. Beyond the south wall the hay rick had burned out, but it continued to smoke, and that smoke mingled with the acrid pall of powder smoke produced by the storehouse explosion.

The Indians seemed to have withdrawn from the station grounds, but Tom couldn't be sure. He couldn't see the corral's far side. He stepped on something. It was Private Peel. Tom knelt. Peel was dead, head lying in a puddle of blood, eyes staring out of his perpetually dirty face. By the corral gate, Tom came upon station attendant Hicks, dead as well.

Tom swore to himself, wiping his mouth with the back of his hand. Should he have ordered the withdrawal to the station house sooner? Maybe. He couldn't change those orders now, though. He remembered what Hayward had told him—not to worry about it, and concentrate on the job in hand. Concentrate on making the right decisions next time.

He entered the station house. The shuttered room was dark and smoky; it reeked of sweat and black powder. With his heart in his throat, Tom searched the gloom until he saw Annie. She appeared unhurt. Tom let out his breath with relief. Their eyes met. He wanted to run over and take her in his arms, and he knew that she wanted him to do it, but he could not. That was the price of being in command.

Hayward was by the back door; he seemed to have taken charge. "What are your casualties in here?" Tom asked him.

"Sanders is wounded, sir—but not bad. Dutch and Cuddy got separated on the way back. Don't know where they are."

"They're not next door. Hicks and Peel are dead. I've no idea what happened to that blacksmith. Sergeant Anders is out of action with a busted shoulder. I'm making you temporary sergeant again, Hayward."

"Yes, sir." Link took the news without emotion. He was blackened and bleeding from the powder explosion. His clothes had been half blown off and he had a terrific headache.

Tom's throat was dry and irritated from the smoke. He wanted a drink, but there were other things he had to do first. They were all looking to him for answers. He wondered if Hayward felt fear at their situation; sometimes he wondered if Hayward felt anything. To his new sergeant he said, "Go next door and tell them to come in here. This is where we'll make our fight, if there is one." Because the carbine ammunition was nearly gone, Tom wanted all the civilian repeaters in one room for firepower in case of another attack.

"Yes, sir," Link said, and he went out.

Tom crossed the room to where Annie stood by a front window, the dead lumber cutter's Henry repeater in her hands, the satchel of money at her feet. He looked into her dark eyes, trying to control his emotions, trying to observe the proprieties. "Miss Bell? You're . . . you're not hurt?"

She smiled, her teeth even whiter than before in her smoke-blackened face with her hair all awry. Her white blouse was filthy and stained with sweat. "So far," she said.

There they were, Tom thought, pretending they weren't interested in one another, when at least half the men knew that they were. Society's conventions were so absurd. "I . . . I'm glad," he stammered at last. Then he added, "I'm very glad."

She laid a hand on his arm. "Thank you, Lieutenant. I'm glad you're safe as well."

Tom cleared his throat and turned away as the rest of the men came in from Bisonette's house. "At least they didn't hit you in the ass this time," Link told Skull as he helped him through the door.

"They did not hit me in the ass last time. I told you—it was my hip."

The newcomers made for the water buckets—Tom was glad he'd had those buckets brought in. The reporter Kimball emerged from his hiding place under the table and dipped a tin cup into one of the buckets as well. Annie put down her rifle and helped tend the wounded, bandaging Skull's shoulder, making a sling for his arm—it was all that could be done for him for now. She washed the blood from O'Meara's face and wrapped a length of cloth around his forehead, covering the jagged wound across his temple. The Irishman's uniform was in tatters from the explosion and his eyebrows were singed off. "Look at me," he said. "A rare sight I must present. Perhaps I could play tragedy now—Lear, or Banquo's ghost."

"You'll be playing your own ghost if this keeps up much longer," said Hunter, who sat against the wall nearby. "It's a miracle we're alive as it is. If that powder hadn't gone up, we'd all be dead right now."

Nearby, the Professor and Harry examined Kiah's ankle. "You're lucky," the Professor said, probing the wound with a finger. "The bullet went clean through, the bone's not smashed. You're going to keep that foot."

"See?" Harry said. "I told you you weren't going to die. Tomorrow you'll be writing your sister, telling her what a hero you were."

When Annie was done with O'Meara, she joined Tom beside Barnacle Bill Sturdivant. Sturdivant's forehead and cheeks were burning; Annie cooled them with a wet cloth. "How are you doing?" Tom asked him. It was a stupid question—the boy was dying—but what else could he say?

The ex-sailor looked up. His breath was labored. Tom could only guess the pain he must feel. The flesh seemed to be melting away from his face. His teeth appeared to have grown bigger and his eyes had sunk; the outline of his skull showed through his skin. He could no longer manage his cheerful grin.

"The bandage has to be changed," Annie said. "I'll do it."

Tom nodded. He patted Sturdivant's shoulder and stood. At last he permitted himself a drink from one of the water buckets. "Sergeant Hayward."

"Sir?"

"Take three men around the corral yard. See where the Indians have gone. See if you can find the missing men."

"Yes, sir."

"Be careful."

"I'm always careful, sir," Link assured him. He turned. "Hunter, Professor, Mad Dog—come with me."

Hunter groaned as he took his carbine and followed Link outside. The moon had set. Much of the smoke had blown away. The few fires still burning gave little light to the ghostly scene. There were vague lumps scattered around the yard, which Link thought must be animals or men. Somewhere a wounded horse was crying. Link motioned with his hand and the little group started off, keeping to what remained of the walls.

Inside, Pennock rummaged through the store shelves, using his big hunting knife to hack open cans of beef and oysters and vegetables, scooping out the contents with his fingers and wolfing them down. After some hesitation, Kimball joined him, opening his food with a pocketknife. Kiah and O'Meara fell asleep, sprawled on the floor. Bisonette sat on the long table, pipe jammed in his mouth. "You didn't need no patrol," he complained. "Those Injuns are gone. They have to be. They got the horses, that's what they came for. It's what they always come for." He drank from a tin cup of water, then stared at it disdainfully. "I wish to hell there was some whiskey around here. Stupidest thing I ever did—letting you soldier boys get rid of good liquor like that. I still intend to get my money back from the government—don't think I don't. You'll pay for that grub you're eating, too—what's wrong, couldn't you find no more onions to steal?"

Annie bandaged young Pemberton's wounded neck and hand. "You're shaking," she said. "Calm down."

"I can't," the gangly telegrapher said. "I just want this to be over. I'm scared to death of Indians. I never wanted to come out here. I just wanted to learn the telegrapher's trade—I even went to school for it. It was the company that sent me here. Said I didn't have a choice. I wanted to work near home."

"Which is where?" Annie asked in a soothing voice.

"San Francisco."

"I've never been there."

"It's a nice town."

"So I've heard. I'm sure you'll get back there soon."

At that moment Link's patrol returned. "The Injuns are still out there," Link told Tom. "They've pulled back from the station about a half mile. Took their dead and wounded with 'em. I saw 'em from the roof of the stable. It's like before—there's a big group of 'em by one of the fires, pow wowing about what to do next."

There were moans from around the room. "And the missing men?" Tom asked Link.

"All dead, sir—the blacksmith, too. Their weapons and ammunition were taken."

Tom nodded. "Thank you, Sergeant. Good work."

Before Tom could say anything else, Kimball appeared at his elbow. The little reporter's bushy hair was unkempt, and his eyes looked big through his thick glasses. "We could ask for terms of surrender," he suggested.

Tom and the others stared at him, and he went on. "It's no disgrace. We've put up a good fight."

"What do you mean, *we*?" Hunter growled.

Tom said, "You've got the wrong war, Mr. Kimball. There's no surrender out here. There's no quarter—on either side."

"That's what makes it so interesting," Link added with a grin.

Kimball looked ill. Just then a sniper's bullet came through the open back door, passing between Tom's and Kimball's heads. Both men dived for the floor, with Kimball scrambling back under the long table.

"Shut that door!" Tom cried as more shots sounded from all around, but Harry Winston had already kicked the door closed.

"They're back in the corral, sir," Hunter said. "Permission to open fire?"

"Denied. No firing until I give the word. We have to make every bullet count."

There was a thud as something hit the station house's sod roof, then another. More thuds sounded against the building's walls.

"Fire arrows," Link said, looking out.

"Now you see why they built this place of adobe," Bisonette remarked as more of the burning missiles hurtled harmlessly at them.

Tom looked back at Annie. He saw in her eyes that she knew the reality of their situation and that she was prepared to face it. "We'll wait till they attack," he announced. "We're almost out of rifle bullets. We'll have to fight with pistols." He paused. "I'm afraid one more rush will overrun us."

Bisonette looked from Annie's satchel to the back of the bar. He licked his lips like he was making a decision. Then he said, "I guess it's time I told you about the bolt hole."

30

Everyone stared at Bisonette. Outside, the rifle fire and the thud of arrows against the building slackened, but no one noticed.

"What do you mean, bolt hole?" Tom asked.

Bisonette went behind the bar, motioning Tom to follow, which he did, along with a few others. "Most of the stations on this line have one," Bisonette explained. "It's a last resort in case something like this happens. This station was overrun so many times before I came here, they called it Burnt Ranch." He laughed, but no one laughed with him.

There were floorboards behind the bar, ostensibly to keep the barkeep from standing in a swamp of spilled whiskey and beer. Bisonette pulled a section aside, revealing a square hole leading underground, with a ladder on one side.

"Where does it go?" Tom said.

"Comes out in that ravine about a hundred and fifty yards east of here, behind a screen of brush and rocks."

"Why didn't you tell us about this before?" Tom demanded.

Before Bisonette could reply, Pennock said, "You son of a bitch. You was planning to skedaddle out of here by your lonesome and leave the rest of us to die."

"I never was," Bisonette retorted. "I just never figured it would come to this, is all. And if I *was* planning to run, why am I telling you now?"

Pennock was stumped by that one.

Hunter spat. "That tunnel's liable to land us smack in the middle of them redskins—there's so damn many of 'em."

"Aye, who's to say they're not at the other end, waiting for us to crawl out?" O'Meara added.

The Professor said, "Who's to say the tunnel's even any good? You tried it, Bisonette?"

"No," the station owner admitted, "but Emory went through it right after I bought this place, and he said it was all right."

"How long ago was that?"

"About two years."

"We had heavy rains last spring," the Professor said. "What if the tunnel's caved in? We could be buried alive down there. I don't fancy suffocating."

In the corral yard there was a rumbling and squeaking

of wheels, along with the jabbering of voices in low tones.

"What's that?" Annie said.

Link peered through the back door loophole. "They're taking the wagon from the stable."

The rumbling diminished as the Indians pushed the old Studebaker hay wagon over the ruins of the south wall and away to the west.

"Injuns'll steal anything, won't they?" Pennock said, shaking his head in amazement.

Tom had an idea why the Indians wanted the wagon, but he kept it to himself. He looked at Link and saw that Link had the same idea.

His thoughts were drowned out as a blast of rifle fire hit the building.

"Here they come!" Link cried.

The men and Annie turned to the windows and doors. Kimball hid under the table. Through his window shutter, Tom saw dark shapes rushing the station house.

"Fire!" he yelled.

Soldiers and civilians opened up. There were flashes in the darkness, drifting powder smoke, screams from outside. The Spencers were quickly emptied. Tom took the Henry repeater and its ammunition from Annie; Link took Pemberton's. Along with Bisonette's repeater, that made two rifles in front and one in back, with Annie and the rest of the men firing pistols in relays through the remaining openings. Above the firing they heard yells and crashes as the Indians broke into Bisonette's house and looted it.

The repeaters' bullets were going quickly, too. "Find some ammunition!" Tom cried to Bisonette as he reloaded.

"There isn't any more!" Bisonette yelled back. "It blew up with the storeroom!"

The din in the small building was tremendous. The two parties were trading shots at almost point-blank range. A bullet ricocheted off the heavy fireplace shovel, went under the table and penetrated Kimball's brain, killing him instantly. Link had a good laugh at that; so did Hunter.

Beneath the crackle of gunfire came a deeper, heavier sound—the rumbling of wagon, fully laden. Across the road there was a spark, then a flame. The flame spread rapidly. As Tom had feared, the Indians had filled the wagon bed with dry prairie grass. When the wagon was a roaring bonfire, a gang of Indians brought the vehicle forward, some pulling it by its tongue, others pushing from the sides and behind.

"Shoot them!" Tom yelled.

He fired the Henry at the Indians as fast as he could lever shells into the chamber, and when the rifle was empty he drew his pistol and fired that. Bisonette did the same, and Annie and the other men blazed away with pistols. Some of the Indians dropped, but the wagon's momentum could not be slowed.

The rumbling noise increased. "Look out!" Tom cried. Pennock and Hunter jumped away from their positions at the front door just as the burning wagon crashed into it.

The wagon came halfway through the door and stuck, bringing down a pile of adobe bricks with it. The house was filled with fire and smoke and adobe dust, with yelling Indians just behind. The men were coughing and choking, half blinded and starting to panic. Indians were shooting through the windows and doors.

"The bolt hole!" Tom shouted above the din. "Now! Hayward—you're first, with the wounded. Take one man with you."

"I'll go," Harry volunteered, leaving his place at the front window. His empty carbine was already hooked to its sling.

"Get all the lamps you can find and light them," Link told him.

The Professor helped Harry with the lamps, while Link peered down the dark, square hole and called the wounded. "Skull! Sanders!" To Tom he said, "Sir, we're going to need help carrying Barnacle Bill. Maybe Hunter—"

"No," Sturdivant said, shaking his head weakly. He looked at Tom. "Leave me, sir. I'm not going to make it anyway. Just give me a couple pistols."

Tom hesitated. "All right," he said. He gave Sturdivant two pistols that had belonged to some of the dead men, making sure they were loaded. Around him the shooting was an ear-splitting racket. Bullets were flying everywhere, and Tom wondered why everyone in the house wasn't killed.

Harry was finished with the lanterns. He handed one to Link, who slung his carbine and started down the ladder. Harry helped Skull onto the ladder next.

"Hurry," Tom said, reloading his pistol.

Dizzied by the pain in his shoulder, Skull made his way awkwardly down the ladder, with Link giving him support from below. Kiah Sanders followed, wincing every time he put weight on his wounded ankle. Harry went after him, guiding himself by the dimming light from Link's lantern.

Tom cried, "Annie—you're next."

Carrying the satchel full of money, Annie moved close to him. "I'm going with you."

"No, you're not. I go last. It's my job."

"I've waited all my life to find you, Tom Conroy. I'm not going to leave you now."

"Yes, you are." He turned her toward the bolt hole. "Go, or I'll have my men carry you."

She hesitated. Then, with a last look at Tom, she lowered herself into the hole, holding the pistol and the satchel in one hand.

In the house the heat from the burning wagon was unbearable. It was almost impossible to breathe in the fog of smoke. There was a banging on the back door. The Indians had gotten a log from somewhere and were beating in the door. Tom and the Professor fired their pistols through the door. There was a scream from the other side, but it would only be a few minutes now.

"Civilians next," Tom ordered.

Bisonette did not wait to be told. He was already climbing down the hole, close on Annie's heels with the second lantern. Then came Pemberton. The telegrapher was so scared that he slipped off the ladder halfway down and sprained his ankle as he hit the tunnel's packed earth floor.

"Pennock! O'Meara!" Tom said.

The two men left their positions. Then Pennock laid down on the floor. "Pennock, you dumb fuck, what are you doing?" his bunky Hunter yelled from across the room.

O'Meara knelt beside Pennock and rolled him over. There was a small hole in Pennock's chest, with blood welling out. "He's shot, sir," O'Meara called.

"Dead?" Tom asked.

"Not yet. He will be soon."

"Leave him," Tom ordered. "Get going, O'Meara. Woodruff—you, too."

The Professor left his place at the back door and dropped down the hole behind O'Meara. The back door was splintering now. In front the Indians were digging away the building's adobe walls brick by brick.

"Campbell!" Tom said.

Hunter fairly leaped into the bolt hole, so anxious was he to get away. That left only Tom and Sturdivant in the room. Tom fired two more shots through the disintegrating back door, then grabbed the last lantern. Behind him the door cracked loudly. The end of the log punched through.

Tom looked at Sturdivant lying against the wall, calmly waiting with the two pistols. "Good luck, son."

"Luck to you, too, sir. Now, get going."

Tom dropped into the hole. Balancing the lantern on a rung of the ladder, he pulled the floorboards back over the opening, concealing it. Above him he heard the back door give way and the triumphant yells of the Indians as they rushed in.

31

Ambrose Sturdivant lay propped against the station-house wall. The bullet in his gut was like a red-hot poker. As he watched the back door being battered in amidst smoke and flames, other visions flitted across his memory: of his childhood in Rhode Island, happy times where it always seemed to be summer; of the day he walked into town to sign on for his first sea voyage; of tropic sunsets and throbbing native rhythms; of his first time aloft in a storm; of all the women he would never know and the family he would never have.

The back door shattered and the Indians burst through, painted and feathered, yelling and shooting around the empty room where they supposed the soldiers must be. Then they stopped and looked around in amazement, as other warriors entered through the windows or the holes they had dug in the walls.

Calmly, Sturdivant raised his pistols and began firing them into the crowd of Indians. Two of the Indians dropped. As Sturdivant continued to fire, the other Indians turned and blasted him with a hail of rifle and pistol bullets, riddling him. Sturdivant managed to squeeze off one last shot, a harmless one into the floor, then he fell over.

In his mind's eye it was always summer.

Sliding Down Hill could not believe what he saw. Along with the soldier they had just killed, there were

but two other bodies in the lodge—that of another soldier, and of a little man who seemed to have been hiding
under the table. Sliding Down Hill's stomach grew cold.
He had been against further attacks on the white men's
camp. This was a bad omen.

Just then Man Alone entered the lodge through the
shattered door, carrying his heavy rifle. Seen through
the thick smoke, and by the flickering reflection of the
flames from the burning wagon in the front door, Man
Alone's black-painted face with its red highlights looked
terrifying, unearthly. He might have been a messenger
from the spirit world.

"Where are they?" Man Alone demanded.

"Gone," Sliding Down Hill said. The white men's
smell—rank and salty—was so strong in the room that
he turned up his nose.

"That is impossible," Man Alone said.

"Perhaps they were never here," an Arapaho warrior
suggested.

"They were here," Man Alone assured him. "We
saw them in the yard, we saw them shooting from the
windows. Three men could not have fired so many
guns at once. There was a woman with them, as well,
I saw her when we attacked their wagon." He waved
an arm around the room at the typical heap of white
man's litter—bits of clothing, shell casings, paper car-
tridge wrappers, tin cans, playing cards and chips.
"Look at their leavings. This proves there were more
than three."

"Then where are they?" asked the massive Sioux,
Gall.

"Vanished," said the Northern Cheyenne war chief
Tall Bull. "They have great medicine."

Man Alone disagreed. "They have not vanished. They
are men, not workers of magic."

Sliding Down Hill had a bad feeling. "But they are
not here, Man Alone. They did not run from the lodge.
We would have seen them."

"Then they dug their way out, my young friend. It is the only answer. Search the lodge. Leave nothing unturned."

Coughing in the smoke, the frustrated Indians began tearing the lodge apart, looking for clues to the white soldiers' disappearance. They rooted along the walls and under tables. Man Alone and Sliding Down Hill, along with some others, tore through the place where the white men served whiskey to each other. There was broken glass everywhere, and several of the Indians cut their feet and hands. In anger they began ripping the planks from the floor and throwing them. When Man Alone tore up one of the planks, a group of them came apart in a square section, revealing a hole beneath his feet.

"Hee-yaa!" he crowed.

The rest of the Indians gathered around, peering into the black hole.

Man Alone pointed to the still-burning wagon. "Make torches! Quickly!"

32

The fleeing whites hurried through the tunnel. Link was in the lead, lantern in one hand, pistol in the other. The tunnel was just wide enough for one man to pass, low enough that a tall man like Link was forced to bend his head. The sides and ceiling were shored up with cedar posts.

From behind and above them came the dull boom of a gunshot, then another. These were followed by a flurry

of shots, then, after a second, one last booming reverber-
ation. Then silence.

"Keep moving," Tom said from the rear of the column. There was urgency in his voice.

The tunnel was cold and clammy; the earthen walls
dripped. In the lantern's dim light, rats and giant beetles
scurried across Link's path. Link hated confined spaces.
Post guardhouses, especially those with individual cells,
drove him crazy, though he made sure that he never let
it show.

Behind Link, Skull struggled along, with Kiah Sanders
hobbling after him. Next came Harry Winston; then Annie, who was all too aware of Jules Bisonette behind her.
It was as if the station owner was trying to see how
close he could come to her. After what had happened between them earlier that night, Bisonette's proximity gave
Annie a creepy feeling.

There was a gap between Bisonette and Pemberton,
whose sprained ankle was swelling grotesquely over the
top of his shoe. The young telegrapher cried with each
step—out of pain, or fear, or both. After him came
O'Meara, the Professor, and Hunter.

"Hurry up, can't you?" the Professor muttered to no
one in particular. "It'll be time for my discharge before
we get out of here."

Tom came last, with the third lantern. Every few steps
he looked back over his shoulder. The pounding of his
heart seemed to echo off the tunnel's narrow walls. Suddenly he banged into Hunter, who had come to a halt in
front of him.

"What's wrong?" Tom said. "Why have we stopped?"

"Blockage." The word came down the line, and everyone's heart went cold.

Tom tried not to panic. "Rest easy," he ordered.
"Don't use up more air than necessary."

Up front Link dug frantically at the wall of earth in
front of him. His cumbersome carbine and its sling got

in his way, but he couldn't get rid of them. The army would charge him for lost property.

Harry squeezed by the two wounded men and joined Link. "Take a break," he said. "My turn."

Link backed away from the blockage, breathing hard, while Harry pulled at the dirt and fallen timbers. "Why the hell do I always end up with you next to me?" Link complained.

"Because I want to make sure I'm there when the Indians finally get you," Harry told him.

"Fat chance of that," Link said. He shoved Harry aside and resumed digging.

Suddenly he was through, almost falling through the hole. "Come on," he told the others.

Link and Harry helped Skull crawl through the narrow opening in the blockage. The big Dane must be in agony with his shattered collarbone, Link thought, but he didn't cry out. They assisted Kiah next, then moved on, leaving the others to follow.

Annie wiggled through the opening, pushing the pistol and the satchel full of money ahead of her. She felt a hand on her leg. "You bastard," she whispered to Bisonette. "Didn't you learn—?"

"It was an accident," Bisonette said, grinning evilly in the lantern light. "Sorry."

Annie kept going, with the station owner still right behind her.

Tom was the last one through the blockage. Then he stopped. Had he heard noises back there? He couldn't be sure. Was it Indians, coming after them? Or rats? Or his imagination? He pulled down more of the wall and the cedar supports, reblocking the passage. If anyone were following, that would slow them up.

Up front Link kept going. Sweat poured down his unshaven jaws, mixing with the dried powder smoke and dirt already there. His back hurt from keeping his head bent. It was getting hard to breathe in the stale air. His lantern began flickering, the light dimming.

Then it went out.

Link swore and pushed forward, feeling his way in the dark, fighting down the fear that they might be trapped in here, buried alive. He rounded a bend in the tunnel. As he did, a feather of fresh air brushed his cheek. The fresh air grew stronger. There must be an opening ahead. Link could make it out now, a vague lightening against the absolute blackness of the tunnel.

He put down the now useless lantern and moved ahead cautiously, pistol ready. Almost before he knew it, he emerged from the tunnel behind a screen of brush and boulders, just as Bisonette had said.

"Wait," he whispered to those behind him.

Quietly he pushed through the brush. He was about halfway up the side of a ravine. There were no sounds; there seemed to be no one around. A dull red glow came from the direction of the station house. There was a lot of yelling back there along with the confused galloping of horses.

Link waited a long minute, crouched, every sense alert. At last he stuck his head back into the tunnel.

"Come on," he said.

33

The others filed out of the tunnel. Link motioned Harry up the ravine to keep watch. He sent O'Meara across the ravine and Hunter toward the river. He himself crept quietly to the ravine's top, looking back toward the station house.

After a minute Link returned, sliding carefully down

the ravine's side until he stood next to Tom. "All clear, sir," he said in a low voice. "They're pretty stirred up back there, though. Looking for us, I expect."

Tom nodded. "We can't stay here. I'm afraid they've found the tunnel. They'll be right behind us. We'll make for the river, there's good cover there."

"Why don't we split up?" Bisonette suggested. "There's a chance at least some of us would survive that way."

"No," Tom said. "We stay together."

"But—"

"That's final," Tom said.

Annie said, "How long before we can expect help?"

"Too long to make a difference," Tom told her. "The crew at Monument Station may have seen the fires here, if anyone at Monument Station is still alive. But they have no telegraph relay, they'd have to send a rider to Fort Pierce. We couldn't expect help before tomorrow evening at the earliest. If they didn't see our fires, tomorrow's stage and escort could ride into a trap, but there's nothing we can do about that."

Tom looked toward the east, where a thin gray line on the horizon showed that dawn was finally at hand. "Let's get moving. I'll lead. Sergeant Hayward, you bring up the rear."

"Yes, sir," Link said.

"Call in your pickets."

Link brought back Harry and the others. "Single file," Tom ordered, "wounded in the middle. Stay quiet as possible. Ready? Move out."

They started down the rocky ravine bed toward the Smoky Hill. Tom went first, with Annie a step behind. The sky was lightening noticeably now, which made the footing easier. They were almost out of the ravine when there was a burst of yelling behind them. Indians were in the ravine's upper end. They had found the tunnel, and now they were searching for their escaped prey.

Between Tom and the river in the dim light was a line

of cottonwoods, willows, and bullrushes. Tom intended
to hide his party in the tall bullrushes until the Indians
got tired of looking for them and rode away. He moved
faster. They were almost safe.

As they approached level ground, the little column
strung out. Jules Bisonette eased behind Annie and her
soldier boyfriend. He'd broached the idea of splitting up
as a way of getting the two of them alone, but this would
have to do. He could grab the satchel full of money from
the unsuspecting Annie and sprint off into the dawn, but
that was not enough for him. He wanted his revenge against Lieutenant Conroy. He had sworn to kill Conroy,
and he meant to carry through with that threat. No man
beat Jules Bisonette and got away with it. Bisonette's
only regret was that he would not have time to get the
lieutenant's ears.

He couldn't wait any longer; it was getting too light.
He didn't care about noise. By shooting Conroy, he
would bring the Indians down on the little party, and
Conroy's men wouldn't have time to chase him. With
luck, he could get away while the others were being
killed. His only regret was that he couldn't take the
woman as well. Oh, well, with this much money, he'd be
able to have his pick of women—respectable women,
too, not whores.

He moved closer to Conroy, raising his pistol, aiming
for the base of Conroy's skull. At this distance he
couldn't miss.

Annie saw him from the corner of her eye. "Tom!"
she cried, flinging herself against Bisonette just as he
pulled the trigger, making his shot go wide. She held on
to Bisonette's gun hand for all she was worth. Snarling,
Bisonette punched her in the face with his free hand, and
as she dropped away, he turned to finish Tom. But Tom
had turned as well, and he fired first, hitting Bisonette in
the chest, burning the station owner's shirt with the
closeness of the powder blast. Bisonette staggered back-

ward with an oath, raising his pistol again, crazy with hate. Tom fired twice more. Bisonette grunted, stumbled backward and fell into a buffalo berry thicket.

Tom didn't even have time to see if Annie was all right. He heard whoops from the Indians up the ravine and on the low bluffs. "Run!" he yelled, dragging Annie to her feet. "Make for cover!"

He held Annie's hand as they raced across the open ground toward the cottonwoods. The rest of the men were right behind. From their rear came more whoops and yells, the sounds of horses descending the bluffs. There was no chance of getting to the bullrushes now, much less of hiding in them. The Indians would be on them in a moment. Ahead was a gigantic fallen cotton-wood. "There!" Tom cried. He ran toward the fallen tree, heaving Annie over one of its monstrous branches, vaulting after her.

"In here," he told the others as they scrambled after him. "Form a perimeter." Link was the last man in, rolling under one of the tree's huge branches.

There was room among the fallen tree's trunk and branches to provide some cover for all of them. It would have to do. Through the intervening screen of trees and undergrowth, they could see the Indians now in the gray-ing light, pursuing them across the flats and into the brush, abandoning their horses.

"Ready," Tom ordered. "Don't fire till they're right on top of us." To Annie he said, "Stay close to me."

She looked up at him. "So you can shoot me at the end?"

"Yes," he said.

He held her gaze for a moment, then he looked around. Everyone was here but . . . "Where's Pember-ton?" he cried.

"Christ," Link said, pointing. "There he is."

Charles Pemberton was stuck in a mass of thorn-bushes—he was a city boy and did not know what they were called. He had blundered into them during the dash for cover, and now he was trying to get out. His swollen ankle was killing him, and he wondered if it was broken. The more he tried to extricate himself from the thorns, the more entangled he seemed to get. He was tearing himself to pieces, yet he barely felt the pain because of his fear.

At last he ripped himself free, tripping over some kind of root, clothes and flesh torn off in long strips, blood flowing, salt sweat stinging the wounds. He stumbled toward the rest of his companions, then stopped.

He was face-to-face with an Indian.

The Indian had a long, sad face and a big nose, and he wore a shapeless old Jeff Davis army hat with a feather stuck through the top. He was carrying a rifle and a war axe, and he looked as surprised to see Pemberton as Pemberton was to see him.

The two men stared at one other. Pemberton's pistol was in his hand, but he was shaking so badly with fear that he could not raise it. He had never been this close to a hostile Indian.

He swallowed and tried to say something to the Indian, but no words came from his parched mouth. He tried to run, but his legs wouldn't work. He heard the soldiers yelling at him to run, to shoot, to do something, but he was paralyzed by fear. At last the Indian ended the impasse, raising his axe and crashing it down into Pemberton's brain.

"Damn." Tom swore helplessly as he watched the telegrapher's death.

At that moment the Indians attacked. They advanced through the trees and heavy undergrowth on foot, hard to see even in the full dawn. Tom's men waited behind the thick branches of the fallen cottonwood, back to back in a rough circle. The Indians began firing rifles and pistols. Arrows whistled through the air and chunked into the cottonwood. Bullets gouged splinters. Powder smoke drifted through the thick vegetation, further obscuring vision.

Tom steadied his pistol arm across the tree trunk. A young Indian with a hornpipe breastplate loomed out of the smoke before him. "Fire!" Tom cried. He pulled the trigger and the Indian dropped away. Around him the rest of his men began firing, slowly, conserving what few bullets remained to them. If it hadn't been for the extra ammunition they'd obtained at the station, they'd have run out long before. Annie was beside Tom, her Army .44 now and then booming. It was hard to pick out targets with the noise and confusion and drifting powder smoke. Most of the fire came from the Indians. The white men were saving their last shots for the final rush.

As abruptly as it had begun, the firing slackened. The Indians drifted away into the smoke and underbrush.

Frantically Tom and his men reloaded. Some were shaking; all were hollow-eyed. "Now what?" O'Meara wondered.

"Looks like they want to talk about it some more," Hunter said. Through the screen of undergrowth they saw the Indians filtering back up the bluffs.

"Faith, they like their talk, don't they?" O'Meara said.

"I ain't complaining," said the Professor.

"Everyone all right?" Tom called.

Harry looked around the little group. He had lost track of his bunky. "Where's Kiah?"

Then he saw him, slumped inside a crook of the fallen tree's branches.

"Kiah!" Harry scrambled over the branches, but even before he got there, the amount of blood on Kiah's chest told Harry that he was dead.

"Oh, no." Harry dropped to his knees beside the body as some of the others gathered around. There was an arrow in Kiah's throat, a ragged bullet wound just below.

"Oh, Jesus," Harry said. He cradled the dead man against his chest, heedless of the blood he was smearing on himself.

He remembered something. He fumbled inside Kiah's blood-sodden jacket and pulled out the photograph of Kiah's girl. The blood had not soaked through to the girl's likeness yet, it was only on the photograph's stiff backing. Carefully Harry wiped it dry on his trousers. He looked at the sepia-tinted likeness. A pretty young woman—Kiah had said her name was Sarah.

If he lived, Harry told himself, he would write to her. Later, when he got a furlough or his discharge, he would visit. He had promised, and he had to keep his promise. He slipped the photograph into his shirt.

If he lived. If any of them lived . . .

34

The war party gathered on the bluff, with their leaders in a council circle. Some squatted, some sat their horses. Yellow Bear, the Arapaho, stood on one leg, leaning on his war lance with his left foot balanced on the opposite knee.

Man Alone spoke first. In the dawn light his black-painted face, with its red eyes and mouth, was as unnerving to the council members as ever. "We should go down there and fight with the soldiers again," he said. "This time we are bound to kill them all."

He was right, but there was much unrest around the circle. Sliding Down Hill, the youngest man present, made the first reply. He stood boldly, not waiting his turn, gritting his teeth as he steadied his feet beneath him. The man-shaped charm on his breastplate had been shot away just as he had reached the fallen tree where the white soldiers were hiding, and the bullet had then lodged in the left side of his chest. The pain was intense, but a warrior did not acknowledge pain. Blood dripped down his chest and hornpipe breastplate and onto his breechclout. "What have we to gain by fighting with those men anymore?" he began. "We shall have to fight with them on foot, not on horseback as we would choose. More of our people will be killed, and we have lost many already. There is nothing more to be won here—no horses, no glory. Only death. What do we tell the widows of our young men when they tear their hair and cut off their fingers in grief? Do we tell them their men died not for glory or wealth, but simply for the chance to die? There will be enough widows and tearful parents around the lodge fires as it is."

"A fine speech," Man Alone acknowledged, "but perhaps your wound speaks for you."

Sliding Down Hill stiffened. "I am wounded, but I can still fight as well as any man here, and I would do so gladly, if I had a reason for it."

"We have a chance to win a great victory, is that not a reason? We have a chance to make the white men fear us."

"We have already won a great victory," said the bull-chested Sioux named Gall.

"That is true," agreed Yellow Bear, shifting to his other leg. "Besides, the white man's medicine is strong. They have the power of reappearing."

"That was not medicine," Man Alone told him. "They dug a hole in the earth."

"Perhaps their medicine put that hole in the earth. Who is to say that if we fight with them again, they will not have another hole in the earth, and reappear somewhere else?"

Other men were finding their voices. The Dog Soldier chief War Bonnet said, "More soldiers may come to fight with us. If we leave now, they will not be able to catch us."

"We should have left before this," Sliding Down Hill said. "We can fight with the white soldiers at any time. They are slow and stupid and they are always where we can find them."

"Our friend is right," said the great warrior Tall Bull. "We have taken everything from these people that is of use to us. Let us wait for them to bring us more."

"More horses," Gall said.

"More guns," said Yellow Bear.

"More whiskey," someone else said, and they all laughed.

Sliding Down Hill moved into the center of the circle, directly opposite Man Alone. "If I have a reason to fight, I will do it. But I am not willing to exchange my life for that of a white man. There is no profit in that. I am leaving."

There was mumbling and nodding of heads. Gall said, "I agree with my young friend from the Dog Soldiers. I am going, too."

"And I, as well," Tall Bull said.

"And I," said Yellow Bear the Arapaho.

Man Alone looked at the council members. He knew he could not change their decision. He must travel a long road to change a way of life that stretched back as far as life itself. He had brought these men as far as he could—this time. They were not ready to practice his new ways—this time. It would require patience. But Man Alone had patience. And there would be other days.

"Very well," he told them. "I will go with you. We have fought a good fight here. Let us rest and hunt and sing songs of our victory, and then we will fight with the white soldiers again."

There were nods of approval. Men stood, and the council began to break up. Except for Sliding Down Hill and Man Alone, those who had been on their feet mounted their ponies. They all rode off, singing and shouting to one another, heading toward Tall Timbers or back to the white men's camp to look for plunder.

Man Alone and Sliding Down Hill were left alone on the bluff. Their eyes met. Man Alone nodded admiration for the boldness of this young man who had stood up for his beliefs and turned the council against him. He had once been a bold young man himself. Sliding Down Hill nodded as well, acknowledging the famous older warrior's tribute.

Then Man Alone took his bow from his horse—the bow seemed more appropriate than his rifle for what he wished to do. He notched an arrow to the bow and walked to the edge of the bluff. It was a long shot to the white soldiers' position. The arrow would be spent when it hit; it would do little damage. But Man Alone wanted to send the soldiers a message—a reminder that their war was not finished.

He raised the bow high, drew the string, and shot. He followed the arrow's flight until it landed among the soldiers near the fallen cottonwood. Then he turned to Sliding Down Hill and smiled. "Come, my young friend. Let us leave this place."

He would have helped the wounded Dog Soldier onto his horse, but that would have been disrespectful. Sliding Down Hill mounted, never revealing pain. Man Alone followed him, and the two warriors rode off.

By the fallen cottonwood, the soldiers watched the Indians streaming off the bluff.

"Christ," Link breathed, "they're leaving."

"You mean it's over?" O'Meara asked, uncomprehending.

"I believe it is," the Professor told him. "I believe it is."

"Why?" said O'Meara.

Link was fatalistic. "Injuns got different ways of doing things, lucky for us. If they ever learned to fight our way, there wouldn't be a white man left west of the Mississippi."

Harry gently laid Kiah's body on the ground and rose

with the others. They saw a distant figure on the bluff
raise his bow. "Look out!" Link said.

Hunter hadn't been watching the Indian on the bluff.
He was taking a long drink from his canteen. He finished, wiping his lips. As he looked up, something hit
him hard in the mouth, knocking him backward into the
tree branches. He got up, woozy, his mouth full of blood.
"What the . . . ?"

There was something else in his mouth, too. He
reached in and pulled out his two front teeth. "Oh, shit.
What happened?"

Link picked the spent arrow from the ground. "A part-
ing gift from our friends. Lucky he wasn't no closer, or
you'd be dead."

"Son of a—" Hunter hurled his teeth to the ground
and let out with every obscenity he could think of—and
a few he made up on the spot. Then he remembered Annie's presence. "Sorry, ma'am," he said, clearing his
throat and spitting more blood.

"It's all right," she told him. "If it was me, I'd probably have said the same thing."

Link looked at Hunter closely. Besides the missing
teeth, Hunter's lip was split open all the way to his nose.
Link shook his head. "There goes that winning smile."

"It's not funny," Hunter said. "What am I going to do
for teeth? How am I going to attract girls?"

"What's a few teeth?" Link said. "George Washington
was the father of the country, and he didn't have *any*
teeth."

"He didn't need them. He was married."

"Come see me," the Professor told Hunter. "I'll make
you some teeth."

"I want my own back," Hunter said.

The Professor shrugged and pointed at the ground.
"There they are. Pick 'em up. But if you decide to see
me, do it quick—I'll be gone in twenty-five days."

Dejected, Hunter sat on the cottonwood's trunk. "Typical army bullshit," he said.

While his men bickered, Tom Conroy left the cottonwoods and walked toward the open space at the foot of
the bluffs. Behind him the sun was coming up, bright
and strong. Annie joined him, standing at his elbow and
watching the dust of the departing Indians.

"It's like a miracle," she said. "Like our lives were
taken away, then handed back to us. It's like we've been
given a chance to start over."

"Yes." Tom was almost too tired to talk. He had re-
signed himself to death, and now that he was going to
live, he wasn't sure how to react.

He looked at Annie. Her clothes were ruined, her hair
was everywhere, and her face was black from powder
smoke. "I'm a mess, aren't I?" She laughed, giddy with
release.

"I think you're beautiful," Tom replied. He took her in
his arms.

Annie looked around. "What about propriety?" she
asked coyly.

"The hell with propriety," Tom said. He pulled her to
him and kissed her. She threw her arms around his neck
and kissed him back.

The men saw them and cheered.

35

Early that afternoon, Lieutenant Starke and the rest of
K Company arrived at Buffalo Creek Station. They
brought with them the stage for Denver along with two
wagons containing rations and grain for the horses.

"Excuse me, sir," Link said to Tom as the two men

watched the relief column approaching. "What are we going to tell them about Frazer and Moonlight?"

Tom had already thought about it. "I'll tell the C.O. what happened in private, but officially we'll say they were killed in action. They'll have families somewhere, let them think those two died honorably."

"Yes, sir. And that civilian—Bisonette?"

"The same," Tom said. Strange, but he felt no more rancor toward the man he had killed. His hand still ached from slugging the station owner—had it only happened last night?

"Yes, sir." Link turned to his ragged group of survivors. "What are you clowns gaping at? The company's coming. Form up, and pretend you're soldiers."

The column halted by the ruins of the station. Lieutenant Starke turned to his first sergeant, Cronk. "Get out your pickets, Sergeant. See to the horses and the wounded—and to this lady."

"Yes, sir," Cronk said in his gravelly voice. He turned his horse and began issuing orders.

Starke dismounted. Tom walked up to him and they shook hands. "Hello, Jim," Tom said, trying to act nonchalant. "Glad to see you. We weren't expecting anyone this soon. How did you know we were in trouble?"

"A party of big-game hunters from England was on its way here yesterday when they heard shooting," Starke replied. "They hightailed it back to Monument Station, and a rider was sent to the fort from there. We've been in the saddle since three this morning. The stage from the east was ready, so we brought it with us."

Handsome and erect, Jim Starke looked every inch the cavalry officer, even though he had started his career as an enlisted man. His field dress included a slouch hat, fringed gauntlets, and two civilian pistol holsters. His blue eyes missed nothing as they took in the ruins of the corral, the ransacked station house with the burnt-out wagon still lodged in its door, the remains of the army camp, the bodies of men and horses. "Looks like you had a rough time."

"Pretty rough," Tom admitted. "I didn't think we were going to make it. We wouldn't have, except the hostiles decided to pull out."

"How many were there?"

"Two hundred, two hundred and fifty. Cheyennes, mostly, with some Sioux and Arapahoes. Our old friend Storm was leading them."

Stark pursed his lips. "I was afraid we hadn't seen the last of him. How long have they been gone?"

"Since just after dawn."

Starke stroked his blond moustache. "They could be fifty miles from here by now—or they could be over the next ridge. K Company will accompany the stage as far as Soda Springs, near Denver. There's a platoon from I Company following us; you'll turn over the station to them." I was the infantry company with which K shared Fort Pierce. "We'll take you to the fort on our way back."

When Sergeant Cronk had his guards set and the horses attended to, he organized parties for collecting the dead: Pemberton, Bisonette, Kiah Sanders, Hicks, Useless Peel, the reporter Kimball, Dutch Hartz, Cuddy, Barnacle Bill Sturdivant, Elias Rhinehart, Frank Walsh. They were buried in the open ground southwest of the station, along with the men who had been killed earlier and temporarily interred in the station garden. After that, Cronk started his weary men policing up the station and Camp Conroy.

While this was going on, Starke took Tom's report on the action. The two men sat on camp chairs in the telegraph relay station. The telegraph apparatus had been wrecked by the Indians, but the building was left relatively untouched. Tom had kept control of himself during the battle, but now he found reaction setting in. He had a hard time finishing the report; he was shaking at the end.

"How are you?" Starke asked, looking at him closely.

"I don't know. I—feel bad. So many dead. I feel like it was my fault."

Starke rose and placed a hand on Tom's shoulder. "You did a good job keeping any of them alive, Tom. You should be proud of yourself."

"You said I'd always remember my first command, but I never expected anything like this."

Starke smiled sympathetically. "Neither did I. You did well."

Did I? Tom wondered. And in his heart he knew that no matter how long he was in the army, or how far he rose, he would always wonder. That, too, was the price of command.

There were no fresh horses for the stagecoach and no facilities for its passengers, so it was decided that the coach and its escort would move on as soon as the horses were grained and rested.

The time went by too quickly for Tom and Annie. There was so much to do that they barely got to see one another. When the coach was ready to pull out, Tom walked Annie to it, carrying the satchel full of money for her. Tom wore the filthy white shirt and uniform trousers that he'd had on all through the battle. Annie had cleaned herself up in the creek and combed out her hair. All her clothes had been looted from the wrecked stagecoach by the Indians—white women's clothing being highly prized by them—and there were no female passengers on the new coach, so she was forced to wear what was left of her wine-colored traveling outfit, with Johnny the Deuce's watch still stuffed inside the blouse. Her right cheek was swollen and there was an angry gash beneath her lower lip from Bisonette's attacks upon her.

The coach was waiting. Jim Starke and the rest of K Company were drawn up behind in a column of twos, followed by the ration wagons. Tom and Annie halted beside the coach door. "What will you do now?" Tom asked her.

"Go to Denver and open an entertainment palace, like I planned."

"By yourself?"

"I'm capable."

"Yes. Yes, you are," Tom said. "You know, you could . . . you could stay."

Annie averted her eyes for a second. "I wish I could, Tom, but it would never work out between us. You know that. In the end we'd both be miserable."

"No, we wouldn't, Annie. I swear—"

She put a finger to his lips. "We're from different worlds, you and me. I could never fit in with army officers and their wives. I'd ruin your career. I could never be more than a kept woman, a whore. I could never be more than what I am now."

"I never said I planned a career in the army," Tom told her.

She smiled wanly. "I never planned a career as a whore."

On the coach box the driver said, "All aboard, ma'am. We got us a schedule to keep."

Tom put the satchel in the coach for Annie, then assisted her inside. He shut the coach door, and they held hands through the window. "I'm due for leave soon," he said. "I could take it in Denver."

"You'll know where to find me," she replied with her old ebullience. "I'll have the biggest saloon in town."

On the box the driver cracked his long whip. "Geddup!" he cried. The lines jerked, and the stagecoach rumbled off. Tom and Annie held hands until they were pulled apart.

"I'll be there!" Tom called.

"I'll be waiting," Annie called back.

Annie looked out the coach window as long as she

could. Tom watched until the coach and its escort had
vanished over the horizon.

Then he turned away.

While the stage was leaving, First Platoon's six remaining members were huddled behind the ruins of
Bisonette's storehouse. Sifting through the storehouse's
ashes, Link had discovered a two-gallon cask of brandy.
The brandy had been hidden under a pile of trade goods
and had survived the explosion and fire that had destroyed the building. The men opened the cask's tap and
took turns pouring the fiery liquid down their throats,
drinking as much as they could before Lieutenant
Conroy came back.

Link's blackened face was swollen and crusted with
dried blood. His clothes were in tatters. Only his carbine
sling and troop boots gave evidence that he might be a
soldier. "I knew there was still booze here," he crowed
as he guzzled. "I knew it."

He held the cask for Skull, whose arm was in a sling.
"Most men in your condition would be out cold by now,
Skull," O'Meara marveled. "How do you stay awake?"

"Legion training," Skull said between gulps.

Hunter grabbed the brandy next. "Here, give me some
of that. I need an anesthetic." He cast a dirty look at the
Professor, who had sewn his split lip, borrowing a needle
and thread from Corporal Zimmerman in Third Platoon.
"I hope to hell you're a better dentist than you are a sur-
geon." He poured the liquor in, then let out a howl of
pain as the alcohol hit his empty front tooth sockets.

"I would have warned you about that," the Professor
sniffed as he took the cask, "but you insulted my professional abilities."

O'Meara drank next, then Harry. "Cheer up, Mad
Dog," said O'Meara, who was already feeling light-
headed. "The worst is over."

Harry said nothing. Kiah Sanders's blood was all over
the front of his checked shirt. The picture of Kiah's girl

Sarah—and a reminder of a promise unfulfilled—was inside the shirt.

Link drank again, brandy running down his dirty, unshaven chin. He looked around to make sure Lieutenant Conroy wasn't coming, then he pulled something from his shirt and tossed it on the ground in front of the men. It was a large, neatly wrapped stack of greenbacks.

"Holy shit!" Hunter said, still reeling from the pain in his mouth. "Where'd you get that?"

"From that gambler's carpetbag," Harry said. "It has to be."

"How'd you do it?" Skull asked.

"Yeah," the Professor said. "The lieutenant never took his eyes off that bag."

Link winked at them. "Military secret."

Harry said, "What are you going to do with it?"

"Take it back to Fort Pierce, you lughead, what do you think?" He picked up the bundle and smacked it in his palm. "We're going to go into town and have us a spree. Hell, that's why we joined the army, ain't it—to have fun?"

There were footsteps. Link stuffed the money back in his shirt just as Lieutenant Conroy came around the corner of what used to be the station house. "Ten-shun!" Link barked, and the men struggled to their feet.

The lieutenant stopped in front of them. Without missing a beat, Link indicated the brandy cask. "Drink, sir?"

Tom looked from one man to the other. They were expecting the worst. Drunk on duty—they could get six months in the guardhouse for this, if they weren't spread-eagled or hung up by their thumbs first—and they might get both. It was Tom's duty to turn them in.

He held out a hand for the cask. "Don't mind if I do," he said.